WRITTEN BY SYLVESTER BARZEY

STITCHES

A COLLECTION OF PREVIOUSLY PUBLISHED SHORT
STORIES FROM VARIOUS HORROR ANTHOLOGIES

SYLVESTER BARZEY

SM

To My Little Monster...
YOU CAN DO ANYTHING!

FOREWORD

ARE YOU A FAN OF TALES FROM THE CRYPT?

I was addicted to it; there's a stack of DVDs above my head as I type this. It's an anthology show featuring short horror stories inspired by EC Horror Comics. I developed a profound appreciation for short stories through classics like "Tales From The Crypt" and various anthology movies and series like "The Twilight Zone," "Fear Itself," "Tales From The Hood," and "Masters of Horror."

I grew up immersed in all of that, so when I received an invitation to contribute to my first anthology, I eagerly accepted. Then came another offer, and another. In my debut year as a writer, I participated in three anthologies. I was in over my head, but I relished every moment. Crafting these small, contained worlds where I could unleash chaos without worrying about sequels or reader expectations became a delight.

When I write short stories, it's primarily for my own enjoyment and to hone my craft. The stories you are about to delve into have been gathered from a variety of anthologies I've been a part of since I embarked on my writing journey in 2017. I've also included some flash fiction for those moments when you crave a quick scare, perhaps while waiting in a doctor's office.

Each story provided me with an opportunity to explore something new, and although I wrote them for my own satisfaction, I sincerely hope you find them equally captivating. So, let's delve deep and uncover what lurks beneath your skin.

BLOOD NOTE (FIRST PUBLISHED IN DESCENT INTO DARKNESS)

"It was the biggest night of their lives, the grand finale of their first world tour taking place in Atlanta. The music blared, the crowd went wild, and they stood on the stage as rock gods," he whispered.

Artificial flames flickered in the cool night air, casting an eerie glow. Soft pops and crackles created a sinister backdrop for a story that had been passed down through the years. I first heard it from my older sister, then at summer camp, but nobody could tell it quite like Jonathan. The kid had a knack for spinning tall tales.

Jonathan placed his hands near the fake fire, rubbing them together briskly as he continued, "Blood Note and their lead singer, Alex Ryder, had the world at their mercy..." Jonathan leaned back in his folding chair and snapped his fingers at me. "Hey! Pass me a s'more," he commanded.

I chuckled and glanced at Maxwell, who had chocolate smeared across his chin. "This fool better be talking to you," I said.

Max shook his head, waving his burnt marshmallow back

and forth to cool it down. With a smile, he popped the white, gooey treat into his mouth. "Nope!" he replied.

"Come on!" Jonathan pleaded.

I rolled my eyes and handed him the last s'more that sat on my plate, waiting to be devoured. "Here, but no more interruptions. Finish the story," I insisted.

He took a large bite, and the chocolate wonder crumbled around his lips. My gaze shifted to my empty plate, and I sighed as Jonathan licked his fingers and resumed his tale.

"Every song... no, every note seemed as if it were meticulously crafted by a higher power. In fact, they were the 'Gods of Rock 'n' Roll.' Their energy was otherworldly, their allure unmatched," Jonathan said, devouring the last remnants of the s'more.

Blood Note was my favorite band; in fact, they were everyone's favorite band. They were like The Beatles or Michael Jackson— something that only comes around once in a lifetime. Something you have to see before it's gone.

"People say Alex made a pact with the devil for his fame. Nobody wants to believe it, but it fits perfectly. A young nobody fresh off a Georgia farm, shows up in L.A. and fills in for a sick singer, rewriting rock history with every word that leaves his lips. That kind of thing doesn't happen; not to people like you and me. Within two years, Blood Note was everywhere; you couldn't turn on a radio or TV without hearing them. They had hit after hit, and were in talks of making a movie after their tour. They were burning bright, but everything that burns bright also burns fast. Alex learned that the hard way, and he also learned that the Devil always collects." Jonathan said.

"My mom said that Alex was living on borrowed time. She said he knew his days were numbered, which is why-" Jonathan interrupted Maxwell's eager statement by flicking a pebble into Maxwell's melted marshmallows.

"Did she mention that before or after she engaged in

extracurricular activities with our gym teacher?" Jonathan interjected. "I'm the one telling the story here, fat boy," he said.

We all exchanged glances for a moment, until Maxwell leaned forward and stuffed the marshmallow into his mouth, pebble and all. He swallowed it with a gulp, then thumped his chest and burped.

"Tasty." Maxwell said and we burst into laughter.

Jonathan wiped away tears from his eyes and continued, "Legend has it that after the show, Alex retreated to his private studio in his sprawling mansion in Atlanta. That's where he recorded his first solo song, 'The Old Man,' a haunting tale of Alex selling his soul. The song possessed such power that the devil himself didn't want it heard. So, he came for Alex that very night. The song remains lost to the world, and Alex Ryder perished with his blood-stained guitar in his hands, leaving behind a note that read, 'The devil made me do it.'"

Jonathan had a way of captivating us with his storytelling. Something about his delivery kept us hanging on his every word, and both Maxwell and I were eagerly waiting for more. But none came. We stared at him for a moment, then I burst into laughter.

"Bullshit!" I said.

Jonathan laughed and placed his hand over his heart, "I swear! The devil killed him!" he insisted.

Maxwell and I stood up. "Alex died from a drug overdose. There was no bloody guitar or any of that shit," Maxwell retorted as we began making our way back to the house.

Jonathan grabbed his flashlight and rolled his eyes. "Because you were there, right, lard ass?" Jonathan jibed.

Maxwell spun around to face Jonathan. He had been struggling with his weight all his life, but this year his father had been pressuring him to lose some pounds. He was being sent to a camp for healthy choices, which was just a nice way of saying fat camp.

"Screw you, Jonny! I'm not fat!" Max shouted, then turned and walked into the house. We stood there for a moment, then burst into laughter before following him inside.

"Take it easy, Max," I said, slinging my arm around his shoulder. "Jonathan's just mad that his story doesn't make any sense," I said with a grin.

Jonathan rolled his eyes as he retrieved the sodas from the fridge. He placed them on the counter one by one and looked at us.

"Alright, if I'm so full of it, what about the song?" he challenged.

"What song?" I replied.

I snatched the cold can and popped it open, turning it upside down. I chugged it like I had been searching for its sweet liquid for my entire life, which is kind of true. Soda had been banned at my house this month; my mom was on some kind of diet, and unfortunately, the rest of us had to follow suit. I despised diets; it felt like they were designed to slowly kill people, which is probably why the word 'die' is in it.

"The song he was working on before he died. Where is it?" Jonathan asked.

I chuckled, "Maybe he didn't get around to finishing or even starting the song because, well, he died?" I retorted.

Max started choking on his soda, spitting some of it out as he burst into laughter.

"What the hell, fat boy?" Jonathan said.

Max nodded, still laughing, "That's true! He overdosed. I doubt there even is a song."

Jonathan whipped out his phone and pulled up a video. "What's this?" I asked.

He pushed play and Max and I lead in, "Is it the song?" Max asked.

Jonathan nodded. "Yes, Max, I have the world's most valuable song just sitting on my phone! It's an interview with his girl-friend, Melody." Jonathan explained.

On the screen, a dirty blonde with ice-blue eyes stared right at us. I felt trapped in her gaze. She didn't utter a single word, but I knew I would follow her into hell if she asked.

"She's got some tits on her, huh?" Max said. My head turned towards him, and I smacked his soda, causing it to splash into the sink. Jonathan laughed, and I redirected my attention to the screen.

Her voice had a husky, Southern twang to it. I smiled. "Is she a singer too?" I asked.

Max patted me on the back. "Uh-oh, Richie's in love. Do you have her number? Maybe her address, a list of all her recent whereabouts in the last 24 hours? You know how Richie likes to know everything about his girls," Max teased.

Jonathan stopped the video and laughed, "You're a dick, Max. Richie likes to know everything about everything," he said.

I closed my eyes, not fighting the truth. It was accurate. I had an insatiable need to know things—it was just a part of who I was. It creeped out girls and annoyed everyone else, but I couldn't help it.

"But she was last seen with Alex Ryder. She's buried right next to him," Jonathan revealed.

"Wait! She's dead?" I asked.

Max leaned on the counter. "That's messed up. You were mentally banging a dead girl," he said, sounding disgusted.

I turned my head towards him, a puzzled expression on my face. "Shut the hell up." Then I redirected my gaze to Jonathan. "She's dead?" I asked.

Jonathan nodded solemnly. "Yeah, she hanged herself the night after that interview. She said she wanted to hear Alex one last time," Jonathan explained, and he pressed play on the video.

Silence engulfed the kitchen, broken only by the eerie static emanating from Jonathan's cell phone. The video playing was ancient, dating back to 1992 when Alex took his own life and Melody followed suit. Resting my hands under my chin, I leaned in, captivated by Melody's words.

"No, No." She said softly, "He wasn't anything like that. Alex was sweet and beautiful-" the reporter's laughter cut Melody's statement short.

"Sweet is a stretch, don't you think? We're talking about Alex Ryder!" the reporter interjected, leaning closer as the camera zoomed in on Melody's face. Once again, his words filled the air, "Come on now, Melody. Are we supposed to believe that Alex Ryder, the bad boy of Rock 'n' Roll, was really the boyfriend of the year?" Melody's gaze shifted downward, her hands twisting and folding a napkin throughout the entire ordeal. The reporter's tone softened. "Melody..."

She raised her head, her blue eyes seemingly locking with the camera, and I felt as though she was staring directly at me. I knew it was just a video, but there was an eerie sensation that she could crawl out of the screen and claim my soul. Over-whelmed, she covered her face with her hands, tears streaming down. We were spectators to the unraveling of a broken heart.

I shook my head and walked over to the living room when I heard her sultry whisper, "He wasn't perfect, but even the Devil had wings."

I turned, and our eyes met briefly before the screen faded to black. I wasn't sure if the warm feeling that was engulfing me was love or me pissing myself. I couldn't deny her haunting beauty, even though she had been dead for for the past tree decades; making her more haunting than beautiful.

"So, his groupie gave an interview," Maxwell spoke up, his mouth full of marshmallow. "What the hell does that have to do with his song?" he asked.

"Where the hell are you pulling those out from? Your ass?" Jonathan asked.

I chuckled softly, feeling uneasy, as I laid my blanket on

the living room floor. Jonathan combed his fingers through his curly, brown hair, pocketing his phone before walking away.

"It's not the interview, it's what she did after it," Jonathan explained.

"Kill herself?" Maxwell asked.

"No, fat boy!"Jonathan snapped.

Before we could react, the staircase lights flicked on, and Jonathan's father shouted, "You little brats better get your butts in bed! It's 2 am! I've got work in the morning."

We exchanged glances and burst into laughter. Maxwell rolled out his sleeping bag, and I settled on the floor with a blanket and a pillow. Jonathan claimed the couch, showing no concern for hospitality or treating guests right. In his world, he was the alpha, and we were his pack.

"When Alex died, he left everything to Melody, and before she took her own life, she ordered that all his money be used to keep the mansion standing," Jonathan whispered.

"Yeah, it's near Piedmont Park. I pass by it when I go to little league," I chimed in.

"What's it like?" Maxwell asked.

"Kind of creepy, but it's still standing. It's got a shit ton of vines on it and some broken windows," I replied.

"Well, at least her last wishes were honored," Maxwell commented.

"No one can enter. It's meant to remain there forever, without a soul stepping inside," Jonathan added.

"And I'll ask again, what the hell does that have to do with the song?" Maxwell muttered.

Jonathan rolled over in the darkness, his face hidden from view. However, I knew he wore a million-dollar grin as he spoke, "If no one can go in, fat ass, that means-"

"It's still in the house," Maxwell and I chimed in simultaneously.

Jonathan chuckled and rolled over. "The geniuses have finally entered the chat," he teased.

It was a random sleepover conversation among three naive kids. If I had known that our words that night would unleash the chaos that followed, I would never have set foot in Jonathan's house. But if everyone could predict their mistakes in advance, life would be hella boring.

IT WAS WEDNESDAY NIGHT, and my coach always scheduled late practices on Wednesdays. My mom believed it was an excuse for him to come home at midnight, blaming the team when he was actually seeing the frozen yogurt girl down the street from the park. She had mentioned it more than once, just not to me. Usually, it was directed at some other player's mom before the game started. Sorry, I'm getting off track here. It was late, and my mom asked Coach Mayfield to give me a ride home.

"Kid, why don't you take a few laps around the block? Swing by the yogurt shop, say around ten?" Coach whispered.

I stared for a while, perhaps too long, as he snapped his fingers, questioning if I was paying attention. I wasn't, as my focus had shifted to the sidewalk across the street. There, in his worn-out blue jeans and tattered Braves t-shirt, stood Jonathan.

"Hey! Are you going to give me any problems?" Coach shouted.

My head snapped toward Coach Mayfield, and I shook it vigorously. "No sir! I'll be the best little alibi I can be, sir! You can count on me, sir!" I shouted, clicking my heels together in a mock salute.

Coach rolled his eyes and walked off towards his car, "Ten!" He hollered.

"Yeah, yeah," I mumbled to myself, before turning my attention back to Jonathan or where he had been, because when I looked at the sidewalk again, he had vanished. I dashed across the street, extending my hand as if it could protect me from the road-rage maniacs determined to turn me into a pancake. With some luck and a couple of prayers, I made it safely to the other side. Cupping my hands around my mouth, I called out, "Jonathan!" My hands dropped to my sides as the seconds ticked by without a response. Maybe it wasn't him.

"Limp dick!" Jonathan's voice echoed through the street, causing me to whirl around and hope that no one had overheard. There was no one on the street, just passing cars. I sprinted toward his voice, my backpack swinging wildly in the cool night air. Coming to an abrupt stop, my sneakers screeched against the pavement. I stood motionless, staring at the empty sidewalk before me. I caught a glimpse of the streetlights' glow and slowly took a few steps backward. I wasn't entirely sure, but out of the corner of my eye, I swore I saw him.

It was a fleeting white blur, and I would have missed it if not for his haunting smile. It stretched from ear to ear, a smile I had never seen on his face before. Jonathan smiled occasionally; he wasn't some emo 'death to happiness' kind of guy. But this was different, so different that I fought an internal battle not to turn my head. Thoughts screamed at me, 'Run. Run back to the park. Hell, run to the damn yogurt shop if you have to! Just don't look.'

"You look like you've seen a ghost or something?" Jonathan asked, his voice swimming in curiosity.

I chuckled and shook my head. Dropping my gear to the ground, I disregarded the fear welling up inside me and turned to face Jonathan, who stood on the other side of a massive black gate. His arms were crossed, and he wore a puzzled expression.

"You alright, man?" he inquired, concern evident in his voice.

Nodding, I removed my ball cap, running my hand over my

black waves. "Just tired," I replied, taking a step back to examine the imposing gate that separated us. Despite its age and rust, it stood tall. My gaze focused on the faded gold letters above the chipped black paint, spelling out "A.R." I whispered the letters to myself, extending my hand to touch the cursive inscription.

As my fingertips lightly grazed the cool metal, a chill coursed through my body. My hand quickly came back. Shuddering, I attempted to shake off the eerie sensation.

Jonathan burst into laughter, and I responded by defiantly flipping him the bird. He reached out, rattling the gate with his hands. The metallic clatter echoed through the night, causing me to place my hands on the gate to keep it steady.

"What the hell, Jonathan?" I hissed, my voice barely above a whisper.

"What?" he asked.

"You trying to let the entire city know you're here?" I snapped back.

Jonathan rolled his eyes. "Whatever, you coming or not?" he asked.

"How did you get over there?" I asked.

Jonathan slid his hands into his pockets and grinned, "How do you think?" He teased.

Once again, my eyes surveyed the imposing gate, and I shook my head. "Nope," I whispered.

Laughter erupted as Jonathan mocked me. "Don't be a little chicken shit. It's not that high," he taunted.

Rubbing the back of my neck, I stared at the pointed metal bars of the gate. My gaze shifted back to Jonathan. "Black boy dies during B&E isn't a headline my mom wants to see in the morning. Besides, my coach is waiting for me at-" I began, but he cut me off.

"I found it." Jonathan whispered. He said it so softly that it took a moment for the message to process in my head.

"You found it?" I asked.

"Yes," he said with a mischievous grin spreading across his face.

"You found it!" I exclaimed, my heart racing.

"Shut the hell up!" Jonathan shouted, "Get your ass in here. It's stuck in the recorder and I need help to get it out." he said.

He found it! He found it! The last song created by a rock God was just one high ass climb away. Rolling my shoulders, I dashed forward, leaping into the air. My body collided with the metal gate, and again the rattle of the gate took over the night. I glanced down at Jonathan, who was waving his hands frantically hurrying me along. I strained and grunted, ascending like a determined squirrel chasing a nut. My hand gripped the spare headed tips of the gate, only to be met with a searing pain. When I pulled back, I felt the quick tear of my skin.

"Son-of-a-bitch!" I shouted.

Glancing at my right hand, as a stream of dark red ran down my arm, quickly staining the white shelves of my uniform. Attempting to close my hand, the searing pain prevented it, forcing my palm to remain open. I could see raw, crimson flesh protruding from my injured palm.

"Hurry the fuck up!" Jonathan shouted.

"I cut my hand, asshole!" I hollered back, looking down at Jonathan's irritated face. I rolled my eyes and pushed through the climb with only one hand. This time I avoided the death arrows and maneuvering between them.

"Aim for the grass," Jonathan advised. Following his instruction, I dropped onto the high grassy lawn of the rock God's domain, lying there and staring up at the starry night sky. The pain in my hand intensified, and the blood caused the grass to stick to my arm. My uniform was ruined, and my coach would give me hell, but the wrath of my mom would far worse. But none of that mattered at that moment... Because he found it!

"You okay?" Jonathan asked, extending his hand to help me up.

I rolled my eyes and sat up, "I'm fine, you ass hat. You could have warned me those things were sharp." Slowly, I turned my hand over, feeling my skin tighten as excruciating pain surged through me. Closing my eyes, I bit down on my lip.

"God damn! That thing got you good, man," said Jonathan.

Peeking through my right eye, I could only make out a blurry image of red. I mustered the courage to fully open my eyes and saw the flap of bloody skin hanging from what remained of my palm.

"Oh, shit!" I cried.

My trembling finger pushed the flap of flesh back into my palm, causing Jonathan to avert his gaze to avoid the gushing river of blood.

"Wrap it up with something, that thing is nasty," Jonathan suggested.

Using my left hand, I removed my jersey, slowly pulling it over my head. Tearing it apart, I gently wrapped the fabric around my injured hand, closing my eyes as I tightened the white cloth around the bloody wound. Finally, I rose to my feet.

"My mom is gonna kill me," I muttered, examining the torn and bloodstained fabric of my uniform. It looked like I got mugged outside of Georgia Tech. Which I decided was going to be my story if someone asked me. "These things are expensive," I added.

Jonathan waved dismissively at my words as he headed toward the steps of the house. "Once we get this song, you can buy that lousy little team," he said, grinning.

We stood side by side, gazing at the cracked stone steps that led to a weathered door. The house exuded the essence of 90s rock, with its extravagant features and badass vibe. Two worn and chipped gargoyles stood tall beside the steps, while stained glass windows showcased faded, dark colors and intricate patterns. On the left side of the yard, a naked woman enveloped in rose vines stood proudly, her thorn-inflicted cuts oozing a now-faded shade of dark red.

Guarding the right side of the yard was a large depiction of a monstrous man, wielding two hammers above his head to form an X. At his feet lay another image of the same figure, pierced by railroad spikes and lying in a faded pool of blood. This window had a large hole in it by the right hammer, most likely done by a kid like me. Someone too scared to tell his friends he just wanted to go home and forced himself to do something stupid.

"You coming?" Jonathan asked.

His words ripped me from my internal thoughts and tossed me back into this reality of fear and pain. I clenched my hand, hoping to force the stinging from my flesh, even if it was just for a moment.

Glancing at Jonathan, who had already ascended the stairs to the front porch, I muttered, "Yeah, yeah, my fucking hand hurts."

"You want to head back home?" Jonathan asked.

As I climbed the stone steps, I genuinely contemplated his question. I could turned back and get chewed out by my coach & my mom, or I can continue; risk blood poisoning, get chewed out anyway-and be rewarded with the final ballad of a legend. The choice was undeniably difficult.

"Hell no, I don't want to go home!" I shouted.

Jonathan laughed, and as I joined him, he playfully bowed. "Well then, after you, good sir," he said.

"Thank you, kind sir," I chuckled, grabbing the doorknob with my good hand. The cool metal twisted, and I heard the satisfying click of the door. Giving it a push, I watched as the door moved slightly, revealing a narrow gap through which I could catch a glimpse of the mansion's interior. "It's stuck," I remarked.

"What?" Jonathan said, and he ran his shoulder into the door. I heard a thump, but the only thing that moved was Jonathan, who tumbled back onto his ass. I burst into laughter, "Shut the hell up!" Jonathan shouted, dusting himself off and rising to his feet. "That's weird," he said.

"It's an old house; the hinges are probably just stuck and need some oil or something," I reasoned, leaning closer to the gap and pressing my face against the wood. Moonlight spilled onto the bottom steps of the staircase, but I couldn't see anything else. I pushed against the door again, but it still wouldn't budge.

"No," Jonathan whispered, running his fingers through his unruly brown curls. After a pause, he continued, "That's how I got in." My head turned slowly towards him, and I noticed his confused expression and pale complexion, as if he was about to be sick.

"Are you alright?" I asked.

"Yeah man, it's just freaky, that's all. Come on, we can get in through the basement." Jonathan took off down the steps, motioning for me to follow, "That's where the studio is, anyway." He said.

My attention turned back to the gap in the door, leaning in once again to catch a glimpse. The moonlight shined on the staircase and I leaned in closer to see if I could get a look at what was jamming the door. A sudden breeze grazed my eyelashes, causing me to blink. Before I could reopen my eyes, the door forcefully slammed into my head.

"Son of a bitch," I exclaimed, gripping the point of impact. I glanced at the closed door, then back at the path Jonathan had taken towards the back of the house. My hand was throbbing with pain, and now I had a nice knot on the side of my head.- Tonight was becoming quite the adventure. I took off down the steps and dashed through the yard until I almost collided with Jonathan, just barely stopping myself from knocking him over.

Jonathan wore that infuriating shit-eating grin again. "What the fuck is wrong with you?" he asked.

"Damn door busted me in the head." I grumbled. Jonathan

rolled his eyes and turned toward the open basement door—or was it a cellar? I had no idea what rich people called their lower floors. Leaving me standing in the tall grass, Jonathan proceeded into the house.

"Stop messing around and get in here," Jonathan called back. I watched as he disappeared into the darkness beyond the cellar door. Hesitation engulfed me; if I were to be honest, it had plagued me since I left the park. Lowering my hand from my throbbing head, I took a few hesitant steps toward the doorway.

"Jonathan?" I whispered, but there was no response. The air hung still, devoid of any sound except for the drum solo of my own heart. Taking another step closer to the dark abyss of the cellar, I called his name once more, "Jonathan!"

This time, the cellar door creaked open wider, as if preparing to consume me like a snake devouring its prey. Closing my eyes and shaking my head, I mustered the courage to step into the darkness, following Jonathan's lead. My footsteps reverberated as I descended the stone steps. The moment my foot touched the floor, I felt the suffocating embrace of the darkness.

"Jonathan! What the fuck?" I exclaimed, slowly turning to catch one final glimpse of the light before proceeding. Yet, all I saw was Jonathan, standing there, staring at me with that shit-eating grin. I jumped back, and a faint, eerie cackle escaped Jonathan's lips—a dry, unsettling laugh that made me uneasy. Not like, he might steal my wallet, uneasy. More like, I don't want to be trapped in this confined space with him, uneasy. "What the hell are you laughing at?" I asked and as the words left my lips; I could swear I saw his eyes go completely black.

The lights flicked on, revealing Jonathan standing near the light switch across the room. Startled, I turned my head back to the door, only to find no one stood between me and the steps.

"You okay, man?" Jonathan asked.

"Am I okay?" I shouted before walking over to him. "What

the fuck was that all about? I'm sick of you laughing at me all the time! My head hurts, my hand's cut up. I look like shit, and all you do is fucking laugh!" I unleashed my pent-up anger.

Jonathan raised his hands in defense, his face devoid of any smile. "Calm down. I have no idea what you're talking about."

I pointed towards the doorway. "Popping up and trying to scare the shit out of me, that's what I'm talking about." Jonathan's eyes followed my finger, and then he looked back at me and I noticed his eyes widen slightly. "What?" I asked, confused.

"You're head is bleeding pretty badly," Jonathan said.

I raised my hand and felt the warm, familiar sensation of blood. "Just great," I muttered, bringing my hand down to examine the blood dripping from my fingers.

"Maybe we should go. You're not looking too good," Jonathan suggested.

My eyes rolled, and I hissed, "I could say the same about you." I took a quick look around the fully finished basement, noting the dusty leather chairs, movie screen, and a large white dog statue that resembled something I'd find at my Grandma's yard sale. Jonathan's gaze remained fixed on me until my head snapped to face him. He began walking down a hallway. "It's this way," he said.

I felt kinda bad about snapping on him, but what was I to think? He had been acting weird the whole night. I placed my hand on my head, wincing at the sting as my finger brushed the wound. Clearly, I had hit my head harder than I had initially thought.

"Sorry, man," I apologized as I caught up with Jonathan. He turned around, forcing a weak smile.

"It's cool, man. I'd be pissed too, but I'm not trying to fuck with you. I heard the song, and it was iconic!" Jonathan shouted.

The door swung open, revealing a room with a large glass window that offered a view into a booth equipped with a microphone and a guitar leaning in the corner. On our side of the glass, there were old-looking black equipment and large boxes that appeared to contain reels. The place was filled with an eerie stillness. I stepped into the room and ran my finger across the layer of dust.

"This is insane," I muttered.

"You haven't seen anything yet," Jonathan replied, rushing over to one of the black seats and examining the large control board with its array of buttons and levers.

"Have you told Max?" I asked. He extended his hand, flicking a switch and turning a dial. The large reels began spinning, and a faint buzzing sound filled the air. I turned around, searching for the source of the noise, and noticed two large speakers mounted in the top corners of the room.

"No, there's no service in this place," Jonathan responded.

Panic swept over me as I spun around. No signal meant no calls or texts. I was in deep trouble if the coach tried to reach me. Worse yet, if my mom called the coach and he had to admit, 'Well, I'm not entirely sure where he is.'

"I'm fucking-" I tried to voice my frustration, but the words got stuck in my throat. My muscles tensed, and I felt the hairs on my body stand on end as my eyes registered what was before me. Bloody handprints slapped against the glass. Something had destroyed the control board, leaving it in shambles. Jonathan stood there, grinning at me, but this time, there was no mistaking it. His eyes were pitch-black, and blood streamed from his mouth. He opened his lips, and a river of red cascaded down his shirt.

"You want to see some real crazy shit?" he said, but it didn't sound like Jonathan. This voice was deep and twisted, unlike anyone I knew. It felt like a chorus of voices, an eerie symphony of whispers. Startled, I frantically moved backward and ended up tripping over my own two feet.

As I struggled to regain my balance, Jonathan approached

me. My heart raced, and I screamed, "Get the fuck away from me!" My hands shot up, shielding myself from the macabre madness unfolding before my eyes.

"What the hell is wrong with you?" Jonathan asked, sounding genuinely concerned.

I looked up, peering through my shaky fingers, and saw Jonathan standing there, his green eyes filled with worry. I glanced over at the glass window and found it pristine, devoid of any fingerprints. Jonathan loomed over me, wearing the same concerned expression my mother would have worn if I had lost my mind.

"You okay?" he asked once again.

I slapped my hands along the wall, using it as support to pull myself to my feet. Was I okay? Well, no, aside from being beaten up, I was now hallucinating. I gazed down at my bloodied hand and shook my head.

"Nah, I'm heading home." I stated, turning towards the door, but Jonathan quickly cut me off, standing in my way with his arms outstretched.

"Hold up, hold up!" He shouted.

"What?" I said.

"You need to hear this song, man. It's all set up, all I have to do is hit play." he insisted.

I closed my eyes and let out a deep sigh before reluctantly saying, "Fine."

As I reopened my eyes, Jonathan was back in the large black chair. I watched as his finger pressed a bright red button, and a smoky voice emanated from the speakers.

"Good or bad, whatever you may see, just remember it wasn't me. The Devil made me do it," the voice declared, sending a chilling shiver down my spine. I couldn't swear that my heart stopped, but I know I held my breath as the voice continued. It was Alex Ryder, speaking to us from beyond the grave, and I loved every second of it. And just when I thought it couldn't get any better, the guitar kicked in, and the song began.

> *I saw the raven in the corner.*
> *Crossed the road for the Devil's daughter.*
> *Far more lost than you'll ever know.*
> *'Don't look back, just let your soul go'*
> *Whispered The Old Man...*
> *Oh no.*

But then, a chilling sound interrupted that epic moment. My heart truly stopped this time as I heard my phone ringing. Was it the coach, ready to tear me apart for not meeting him after his late-night snack? Or perhaps my mom, wondering if I died before she could get the chance to kill me for making her worry? My hand instinctively reached for my pocket, pulling out the sleek cell phone. The pain in my chest eased as I saw Maxwell's name on the screen. I raised my index finger, feeling the sting in my hand as the tightened skin reminded me of the injury. I turned around and brought the phone to my ear.

"Max! You won't believe this shit-" I started, brimming with excitement.

But Max's tone and his peculiar question cut my excitement short. "You've seen Jonathan?" he asked, his voice laced with worry. Before I could respond, Max continued, "His mom said he hasn't been home for two days. The cops think he ran away, but he wouldn't do that without telling us, right?" My head slowly turned to look over my shoulder at Jonathan, who was staring at me with an unsettling gaze. The song had come to a halt, and all I could hear was Max's voice on the line. "I don't know, man. Maybe we should go out looking for him?"

"He's, right here." I managed to say.

"What? I can't hear you, man. You're breaking up." Max replied.

I turned around, "He's right-" but before I could utter the last word, Jonathan snatched the phone from my ear and flung it across the room. I watched in disbelief as my once sleek and fancy phone crashed into the wall, shattering into pieces a hoe's dream of being a house wife.

"What the hell, Jonathan!" I shouted.

Jonathan glared at me, his eyes icy cold, piercing into the depths of my soul. He shook his head, and as if under his command, the cellar door slammed shut, plunging the room into darkness. My head spun around to the sound, but all I could see was a dark abyss. When I turned back to face Jonathan, I stumbled back and Jonathan laughed.

"I brought you here to listen to the voice of a God, and you answer your fucking phone!" Jonathan bellowed, his voice filled with rage.

I shook my head; I don't know how wide my eyes got, but I felt I couldn't open them any more if I pried them open with a crowbar.

"Jonathan." I whispered, my hands trembling as they slowly rose in front of me. My heart pounded relentlessly, uncertainty coursing through my veins.

"What did that fat fuck say? He told you I ran away from home? That my mom's worried? He's a fucking liar," Jonathan scoffed, shaking his head. "The fucker is just jealous that he isn't here."

"Jonathan," I pleaded, my voice barely audible. Fear gripped me tightly, my senses on high alert, but I couldn't decipher the truth from the terrifying illusions playing before me.

"I told that fat boy to come with me, and he was all, 'Nah, I can't. My dad would be pissed,'" Jonathan took a step closer, and I instinctively took a step back, retreating further into the darkness. "But not you, Rich. I knew you wouldn't back down. You're my bro 'til the end, right?"

"Jonathan!" I screamed!

"What?" he asked.

"Behind you," I managed to breathe.

Jonathan turned around cautiously, his eyes searching for the cause of my distress. Yet, like me, he wasn't prepared for what materialized before us. It stood there, shirtless and covered in blood, a gold inverted crucifix hanging from its neck. I couldn't tear my eyes away from the gory veins dangling from its slashed wrists, pulsating wounds that spewed blood, creating a pool at our feet.

It snapped its head back and black dreads cascaded down onto its body, "Good evening, Atlanta!" It screamed into the air.

"This can't be happening." I mumbled. Gradually, its head lowered, and a pair of hazel eyes locked with mine. In that chilling moment, I knew exactly who was turning my blood into a river of ice. It was Alex Ryder, not quite alive, but definitely in person. He wasn't anything like I remembered, nothing like the poster that hung on my wall. His long iconic dreadlocks resembled filthy, lifeless serpents hanging from his skull. His once vibrant brown skin now bore a dark, weathered umber shade, as if someone had tightly stretched it, causing cracks to ooze with blood.

Alex's lips parted, and my heart threatened to burst from my chest as I heard him say, "There's always room for one more fan."

The voice boomed with its characteristic stage presence, yet there was an eerie quality to it—a haunting essence that split my being into conflicting desires: to flee in terror or to follow him into the depths of hell. But when he spoke again, every fiber of my being screamed for run.

"Always room for one more fan!" he declared in that same demonic tone I had heard before.

"Oh, fuck!" We screamed in unison, and I witnessed Jonathan darting towards the recording studio. My gaze broke away from Ryder's stare, and I sprinted after Jonathan. Whether it was fear or my baseball reflexes, I swiftly surpassed him, bursting through the open door and racing towards the one adjacent to the glass window. Without slowing down, I yanked the door open. I had no intention of ever looking back. Yet, just then, I heard it.

"Help me!" Jonathan's scream pierced the air.

I spun around to see Jonathan sprawled face down on the floor, his bloody fingers desperately clawing towards the sound room door. "Help me!" he pleaded once more.

I sprinted back and grasped his hands, striving to lift him to his feet, both of us pushing through the pain of our blood-soaked palms. As I examined the cause of our struggle, I saw two thick, bloody veins wrapped around Jonathan's ankles. My gaze followed the horrifying trail these veins created until, once again, my eyes locked with Ryder's.

"Come on, boys! Let's get a little crazy!" he bellowed.

"Fuck, fuck, fuck!" I shouted and broke my eyes away from whatever the hell Alex Ryder had become and I pulled Jonathan, but for every inch I cleared, Ryder yanked us back towards him. Before we knew it, we were back at the studio door.

I dropped Jonathan's bloody hands, "What the fuck!" Jonathan cried. I jumped over Jonathan's body and grabbed the door.

"Show's over, you son of a bitch!" I yelled, slamming the door shut on the thick veins, severing them in half. "Get the fuck up!" I demanded, pulling Jonathan to his feet. Together, we rushed into the sound booth, slamming the door shut and locking it behind us.

"What the fuck is going on?" Jonathan shouted. I was too busy scanning the room and having my internal panic attack to give a shit about him.

"Alex Ryder is fucking trying to kill us! That's what's happening," I declared, my eyes scanning the room frantically.

There were no ventilation ducts or secret escape routes like in the movies. "We're screwed," I hissed

"Alex Ryder is dead!" Jonathan shouted.

I spun around, my finger pointing towards the glass window. "Tell that to—" My words trailed off as my gaze met Ryder's grinning face on the other side. "Him," I muttered. Jonathan and I backed up, knocking over a microphone and a bar stool in the process.

Ryder's hands softly touched the clean glass window, leaving bloody prints as he took his finger and started drawing a circle along glass. I couldn't hear anything beyond the glass, but watching his silent laughter was enough to create a lifetime of therapy bills.

"What's he doing?" I whispered.

"Go fucking ask him!" Jonathan replied. Alex proceeded to draw two more bloody circles within the first one before taking a small step back.

"It's a bullseye," I said. My eyes went from the drawing to Ryder, who had his index and thumb out like a gun, mockingly aiming it at us. Then, I heard a faint shattering sound. "No, no, no!" I shouted as the glass beneath the blood began to crack.

Ryder lunged towards the glass, his head aimed directly at the bullseye, his bloody dreadlocks trailing behind him. In panic, I dropped to the floor, covering my head with my hands. My heart raced, and the throbbing pain in my hand and head intensified as I braced myself for the worst. Suddenly, I felt a hand on my shoulder, causing me to jolt back, knocking over a white guitar that sat in the corner of the room.

"He's gone," Jonathan whispered softly, extending his hand towards me. I stared at his hand, noticing that something had completely torn off his fingernails, they was probably sticking up on the floor somewhere. I retreated until I could rely on the support of the wall to pull myself up.

"Where did he go?" I asked, my eyes fixated on the perfectly intact glass window.

"I don't know," Jonathan replied. I rushed towards the door, my trembling hands struggling to unlock it. "What are you doing?" Jonathan asked.

"Getting the hell out of here!" I bolted toward the studio door. My body came to a full stop, as I stood there staring at the door for a moment. I glanced back at Jonathan, who had slowly made his way towards the door of the sound room. Taking a deep breath, I pulled open the door only to be greeted by an empty, dusty basement—the same sight we had seen before. Without wasting any time, we both sprinted towards the cellar door. My hand grasped the doorknob, but no matter how much I turned or pulled, the door remained stubbornly in place.

"Open the damn door, Rich!" Jonathan shouted in frustration.

"I'm trying!" I yelled back.

"Who's down there?" a voice echoed from the top of the steps that led to the main floor of the mansion. Jonathan and I froze, exchanging uncertain glances. "Hurry! Before he comes back!" the voice urged, its softness managing to offer a sliver of calm amidst the chaos. I darted towards the steps, but Jonathan's cold, bloodied hand caught hold of me.

"Where are you going?" he asked.

I wriggled free from his grip. "I'm getting out of here, come on!" I shouted.

"We don't know who the hell is up there," Jonathan protested.

"Well, we know who's down here." I said, and with that, we raced up the stairs, slamming the door shut behind us. Leaning against the door, I took a moment to catch my breath before turning to face a woman with long, black braids standing at the end of the hallway. "Thank you," I said with relief in my voice.

"We have to hurry!" She shouted. Her back was to us, but her voice seemed so familiar.

"How do we get out of this place?" Jonathan asked.

We ran down the hallway, but with each step we took it felt as if the journey was getting longer. I stopped in my tracks, watching in disbelief as the hallway seemed to stretch out endlessly. Then my gaze fell upon her. She donned cutoff jean shorts that clung tightly to her black fishnet stockings. She had spiked bracelets, a metal chain for a belt and a dirty white crop top that revealed a tattoo on her lower back. As I read the dark curved letters I realized why her voice was so familiar; stamped on her back read, 'Property of Alex'.

"Jonathan, it's Melody!" I shouted.

Melody spun around with crazy speed, her head snapping to the side with a loud crack. That's when I noticed the bed sheet noose she held in her hands.

"Out?" she hissed. The white noose slowly came up into Jonathan's view and and I watched as he froze in terror. "There's only one way out!" She screamed, flinging the noose around her own neck. Her icy brown eyes locked onto me, and a sinister smile spread across her face. This was the third time I locked eyes with death. Melody tugged on the rope., "Going up?" she taunted.

We witnessed in horror as her neck snapped and the noose yank her body into the air. Her legs thrashed, and her body convulsed until she disappeared from our sight.

"Oh, shit!" Jonathan shouted before darting down another hallway. This had to be a nightmare, I told myself. It was the only explanation for the horrors we were experiencing. My heart tightened within my chest, and I placed a trembling hand over it, gripping tightly. If I were a few years older, I might have thought the sharp jolts of pain, meant I was having a heart attack. Maybe I was.

"Jonathan!" I called out as I turned the corner, realizing he hadn't gotten too far. Jonathan stood completely motionless near the end of a staircase, not even his chest was moving, it was as if he had forgotten how to breathe. "Jonathan," I whispered, slowly approaching him. When I reached his side, I understood what kept him frozen in place. There was a lifeless body lying in a pool of blood by the front door.

"That's why the door wouldn't open," Jonathan whispered. I began walking towards the body, but Jonathan's hand tightened on my shoulder. "Don't! It could be them messing with us again," he warned.

Nevertheless, I continued my approach, sensing that this body was different from Ryder or Melody. It appeared smaller and still. As I drew closer, my hand covered my nose, I gagged at the putrid stench of rotten decaying flesh.

"Call the police," I whispered urgently.

"What?" Jonathan asked, confused.

I turned back and shouted, "Call the police!"

"I can't," he replied softly.

"You can still call 911 without service, Jonathan," I hissed, frustration seeping into my voice.

I knelt down, the blood stained what was left of my white uniform. This body was new. This one didn't belong here with whatever was chasing us through this mansion of hell. I placed my hand on its shoulder and gently turned it over. As the body tumbled, I fell backward, landing on my rear. The eyes were missing, brutally gouged out with something sharp and jagged. The mouth was frozen open in a scream. Despite the grotesque face, I recognized who it was. "Jonathan?" I said puzzled.

"I can't let you leave, Rich," a demonic voice echoed from behind me. Slowly, I turned my head to glance over my shoulder. A pale, black-eyed Jonathan grinned menacingly at me. "You've got to stay and party with us! Forever!" he shouted.

Jonathan was dead. He had been dead for days now and this abomination had tricked me into entering this house of horrors.

It played me like a God damn game boy. Leaping over Jonathan's lifeless body, I reached for the door, desperate to escape.

"Where are you going, Rich?" the demonic voice bellowed. I refused to look back. I couldn't look back. This was my chance to break free. Kicking Jonathan's body aside, I yanked the door open.

"You ready to rock!" Ryder screamed.

I found myself face to face with pure evil. Staring into those abyss-like black eyes, I felt the presence of the Devil himself. Fear and panic coursed through my veins, but before I could run or scream, Ryder rammed the spiked neck of his guitar into my chest, hoisting my body into the air.

"There's always room for one more!" He screeched.

THE CITY DIDN'T GO into much of a panic over our disappearance. Kids went missing every day, most people believed Coach was involved. So, when they arrested him, everyone thought that was the end. Open and shut case, just how Atlanta likes them. No one paid attention to Max when he claimed to have spoken to me or that Jonathan had invited him to explore Ryder's old mansion. Nobody listened, so Max, being the loyal friend he was, came looking for us.

"What are you doing here, Max?" I whispered from the mansion's top window.

"How the fuck did his fat ass get over that gate?" Jonathan asked.

"He picked the lock." Melody replied softly.

"Smart," Jonathan and I said simultaneously.

"Well, let's go greet him," Jonathan declared, turning away

from the window and venturing further into the darkness of the room. Melody slowly followed behind him. Meanwhile, I remained fixated on Max, who was slowly making his way up the stone steps.

"We don't have to, we can just pretend we didn't see him," I whispered.

Suddenly, I felt a hand rest on my shoulder. "That would be rude," Ryder said, leaning in close. Our eyes, black and intense, locked as he grinned. "Besides, there's always room for one more fan!"

2

QUICK BITE: DARK FLESH (FLASH FICTION MADE FOR BLACK FAE DAY)

Blood-soaked wings dripped warm droplets from the heavens, and in that moment, I knew my fate was sealed.

"Fly, you are the swiftest among us! Soar now and bring back the King, bring back the armies and wizards—" My mother's voice trembled, her once regal presence diminished by weakness, injury, and the gnawing hunger that plagued us all. From Uncle Randil, whose towering figure boasted shimmering onyx skin, to the twins Twilight and Stardust, whose whispered words revealed the toll the icy cold had taken on their fragile forms. We were the black spots amidst a mountain of snow and ice, fading into oblivion.

"My Queen, his wings cannot withstand this weather," Uncle Randil spoke truthfully, his words piercing my mother's flickering hope. She turned her gaze away from him, her attention fixed on Twilight, whose lips had turned ashen, resembling the remnants of a dying fire.

I pushed myself off the frigid ground and gazed toward the

west. "I will follow the setting sun and return with sustenance by nightfall."

"This land is desolate, Gogu. Nothing thrives amidst the ice," Uncle Randil cautioned, but I plunged my sword into the ground, using it as leverage to stand tall.

"No land is devoid of flesh," I asserted, hearing my mother's desperate pleas for Uncle Randil to accompany me. If only I had known then what I know now, how I wish he had never followed.

FIVE MONTHS LATER

"You must eat," Grandmother insisted, her wrinkled fingers urging me to take the cake into my mouth. Before I could decline, the sweetness crumbled along my tongue, and I recoiled with laughter.

"I'm full, Mama!" I responded, throwing my hands up in playful surrender. Grandma persisted, moving closer with her plate of treats, but like I always did to avoid things I disliked, I took to the sky.

Flapping my wings and slicing through the air, Grandma's words faded into the distance. I soared high above the lush green trees, inhaling the fragrance of cherry blossoms. The warmth of the sun caressed my glowing brown skin, and for the first time in months, I felt genuinely happy to be alive.

"Gogu!"

My name trickled through my ears, and I smiled, thinking of the lips that it lives on. My body twirled through the sky and bolted toward the place my heart called home.

"Ember, sweet Ember. How radiant one can be, even at this hour—"

The door to her cottage stood open, leaning against the inner wall, broken off its hinges. My eyes took in the sight, but it was the bloody handprint on the wood that seized my full attention. My hand reached out towards the bloodstain, my fingers settling within its marks, and that's when I saw her.

Eyes a milky white, she was focused on gnawing through the cartilage of her wings. Her teeth tore at the remnants of flesh, blood sparkling as it mingled with the tattered wing. Gashes ran down the center of her chest, blood and torn fabric intertwined with her skin after hours of rest.

"Ember?" I whispered to no one but despair.

Her eyes snapped up from her wing, briefly meeting mine, before she leaped to her feet and sprinted towards me. Her hands stretched out, her mouth wide, as I watched her blood-stained teeth draw closer, craving the sweet nectar of my flesh.

"Meat!" she wailed.

I swiftly grabbed her outstretched arms and tossed her into the dirt of her front yard. She swiftly got to her feet, teeth snapping in my direction. My hand instinctively moved towards the hilt of my sword, fingers poised around the cool metal.

I gazed at her, my eyes locked in a dance with familiar windows that once welcomed my soul. Within that milky gaze, I searched for the Fae who would rest her head on my racing heart. The Fae who held magic within hidden pockets of her very being.

"Ember," A whisper from the lips of a lover, but as she rushed towards me, screaming for meat and blood, I realized my whisper had fallen on dead ears. The sword was swiftly unsheathed and just as fast as I placed a crown of roses on her head and asked her to be mine... I severed her head from her neck. Her lifeless body crumpled to the floor, yet her decapitated head continued to snap and scream. With caution, I approached her and took hold of her black curly hair in my hands, and then took to the sky, sneaking the only person who could make all things right.

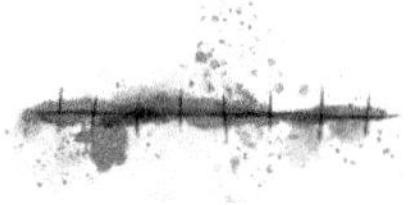

"FATHER!" My panicked voice echoed through the castle walls, but I wasn't the only one calling for him. The twins were bickering at his feet.

"She took it!"

"I did not!"

"You did too!"

"Took what?" My father, the King, knelt down, observing his little miracles—both having survived a perilous birth and the harshness of the ice and snow.

"It!" they screamed in unison.

"What is—"

"Father!" I interrupted, raising Ember's head in my hand. Though her jaw moved sluggishly, it continued to spew curses for flesh and blood.

"What unholy-"

"It's happening all across the Kingdom, Your Majesty," my father's Hand, Sir Bloom, entered hastily behind me. He carefully circled around, eyeing the remnants of Ember in my grasp. "A dark madness has befallen us, resurrecting the dead from the icy embrace of the earth."

"Go find your mother," the King commanded the twins.

The twins slowly rose to their feet, fleeing from the chaos I had brought into our castle. I set the head down on the floor and pointed towards it. "Her eyes were white when I found her, and she was devouring her own wings."

The King approached Ember's head and extended his hand. "Your sword," he breathed. I withdrew my blade and handed it to him, witnessing as he plunged it deeply into the center of Ember's skull. Blood splattered onto my father's face, and then he turned to me, Ember's blood tracing down his cheek. "What is this madness?"

"It's the Dark Flesh, a curse from centuries past," Bloom declared, casting a grave gaze in my direction. "That is what has befallen us now."

My eyes dropped to the bloody severed head that bled at my feet before returning to Bloom. "This must be stopped."

"We have no idea what this is," my father interjected.

"It is the Dark-"

"Preposterous! No one within the kingdom harbors such hunger. Life here is good, easy... There is no need for such barbaric cravings," my father rebutted.

"Then outside the kingdom," Bloom replied.

"Speculation will not bring us closer to a solution. Whatever this affliction may be, the remedy remains the same. Gather the afflicted, confine them in the courtyard until we can unravel this mystery. Enforce a curfew throughout the kingdom—"

"Your Majesty, what about those who won't be easily apprehended?" Bloom inquired.

My father locked eyes with Bloom and then shifted his gaze to me. "The safety of the kingdom takes precedence. Execute all those who refuse to comply."

"The people will revolt. Killing the sick... father-"

"Go see to your mother and siblings," my father interrupted me.

"But father-"

"Go!" he shouted, and I obeyed his command, reminding me of my place. Listening to them speak of the Dark Flesh in hushed voices. The castle halls were silent, devoid of the bustling servants preparing for the day's events. They were likely seeking safety with their families. I arrived at the twins' room and froze. Just as it had been at my beloved's home, a bloody handprint marked the center of the door, albeit smaller this time. My fingers instinctively reached for it, only to have the door violently flung open.

"My son! Come in, quickly!" My mother commanded.

"Mother, what is-"

"The twins are not themselves," she uttered the words so casually that one would think it meant the twins were merely unwell or unhappy. However, as my gaze shifted beyond her to the blood-streaked room, I saw them—two bloody mirror images feasting upon the flesh of what appeared to be their chambermaid. I recoiled in horror, but my mother's hands swiftly covered my mouth, preventing a scream from escaping. "Don't you dare, not after all I've done for you."

I forcefully removed her hands from my mouth. "They are devouring Fae!" I whispered fiercely.

"It cannot be helped! When they sleep, they must feed. They know not what they do," my mother explained, her eyes avoiding mine, weakened by guilt. "If the kingdom were to discover the truth, they would kill us," she added.

"Us? They are the monsters that killed my beloved..." I unsheathed my bloodstained sword and pushed my mother aside. "I will rid them of this darkness myself!" My voice rose, capturing the twins' attention. Their eyes, like my beloved's, were glazed over in white, but they paid me little heed before returning to their macabre feast.

"The murderer you sneak is in this room, but not among the twins," my mother declared.

My sword was at the ready and I contemplated calling my father, but no man should be forced to kill their own children. "I have no time for your games, mother," I hissed. My sword rose, and then she grabbed my arm.

"We don't remember what we do. Some mornings, it feels like a nightmare, and on others, it is as if nothing has happened. But for the past few months, I have stayed awake. I have followed you children and cleaned up your messes," she confessed. She nodded towards the twins, feasting upon the body like savage wolves. "Some messes are easier to clean than others."

"This is madness," I muttered, my hand inching towards the door. She was mad, and they were monsters. As my fingers curled around the doorknob, my mother turned her head towards me.

"When was the last time you ate?" she asked.

"What?" I replied, taken aback.

"The last time you had a meal. Can you remember?" she pressed.

I pondered for a moment and every time I thought I had a memory of a meal; my mind then recalled turning it away. I remembered rejecting Grandma's cake and spitting it out as I took to the skies. Gazing at my mother, I shook my head lightly. "I don't recall," I admitted.

"But you're always full," she added.

"Yes," I confirmed.

"And does that not strike you as peculiar?" she questioned.

"Peculiar, indeed. But this..." I gestured towards the twins, raising an eyebrow. "This goes beyond peculiarity," I asserted.

"The last meal I remember eating was the one in the snow," she revealed, her voice soft.

My hand gripped the doorknob, and I swung the door open. "I'm going to find Father!" I shouted before slamming the door shut and wedging my sword between the handle and the wall, sealing them in.

"Gogu!"

Once again, my name reverberated in my ears, but it was not the voice of my beloved or my mother. I listened intently, tracing the source of the cry through the labyrinthine corridors of my father's castle.

"Gogu!" The voice grew deeper, and the air turned colder.

I halted in front of an icy door, pushing it open with trembling hands. The wood scraped against the frozen floor, covered in a blanket of snow. Crossing my arms over my chest, the muscles in my wings tightened. With each step through the snow, I felt myself transported back to that nightmarish snowy landscape from months ago.

"Gogu!" I turned my head, and there stood Uncle Randil, wearing a blood-stained smile. "All will be well, Gogu. Your father will send for us, and we will survive."

My gaze fixated on the blood trickling from his teeth, and then I averted my eyes back to the snow. "But we need to eat," I whispered.

"The land is barren," Uncle Randil murmured. His hand rested on my shoulder, his frigid fingers inching towards my neck. "Come now, let us return."

"No land is devoid of flesh," I declared. When I glanced back at him, his eyes widened, reminiscent of the day my sword pierced his chest. And then, his body fell apart into fragments of chopped meat—meat that sustained us for five days.

"Gogu!" I turned to the white expanse of snow, where Uncle Randil's head wore a twisted, blood-soaked smile, nestled in a soft mound. Dark red stains formed around him. "Dark Flesh doesn't seem to agree with you, boy!" Randil erupted into laughter. I clamped my hands over my ears, but his maniacal laughter pierced through my skull as if he were screaming from within me.

"Gogu!" I gazed skyward, where my father hovered above me, the moonlight casting an eerie glow on the axe he clasped in his hand. I released a lifeless body I hadn't realized I was clutching, yet the taste of flesh lingered on my lips. Mother had been right—sleep became a gateway to a hell where unspeakable acts were committed. "I'm so sorry," my father whispered, his words barely audible amidst the flapping of his blood-soaked wings.

Blood-soaked wings dripped warm droplets from the heavens, and in that moment, I knew my fate was sealed.

"I'm awake," I whispered, as the axe sliced through the air, its final destination my skull.

3

LISA (FIRST PUBLISHED IN 7 SINS OF THE APOCALYPSE)

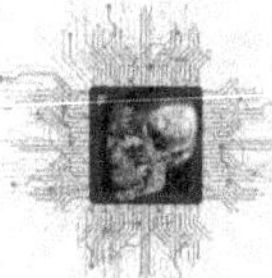

*J*eff, rise and shine. Today is going to be a wonderful day.::

The robotic female voice whispered into my ear and, like magic, my eyes popped open. I sat up and smiled as the birds flew gracefully through the sky.

:: Good morning, Jeff::

"Good morning, Anna."

:: Did you sleep well?::

"Like the dead, and yourself."

:: The dead don't sleep and neither do I. What would you like for breakfast.::

My hand touches my chin and I playfully pretend I'm struggling to decide from a mountain of opinions, but we both know what it's going to be. A scramble made with three whole eggs and two egg whites. Bacon heated to exactly 165 degrees and removed from the pan to rest on an oak cutting board. Two pieces of toast with the edges cut off. Lastly, goat cheese on the side. It's the same thing every day but I always say, "Surprise me."

:: Will do, should I play your messages from last night while you get ready?::

"Yes, please."

:: From Instagram:

@RealTonyHawk "Sick move, man, you're getting so much better. I can't wait for our next lesson."

@CardiB "Press, Press, Press, Press... well you know the rest, thanks Jeff for helping me with that song, it's gone triple platinum!"

From Twitter:

@POTUSTrump "Thanks for getting that weapons bill thing signed by Korea, this is going to be huge! HUGE! For my third reelection."

From Facebook:

Jennifer Lopez liked your most recent post.::

Anna is my A.I Life Assistant. We have synced her to my life, it's a long process that involves smart tech talk and a lot of wires but in the end I get a life worth living.

:: Jeff, you have an incoming call, would you like to answer it?::

I try to think who would call during my daily routine. Most likely Lisa from the office asking me out for drinks after work.

"No, send it to voicemail." Lisa will have to get in line. Besides, I set my mornings in stone, even the slightest misuse of time will throw off my whole damn day. One minute talking to Lisa means one less minute working on my fitness or one less minute to close a deal. I spend the rest of my morning pondering wither or not sex was worth $50,000. I would never pay that much in my life, but if I broke down my day into payments by minutes, that's how much it would cost to get Lisa into bed. I could get a high-end call girl for half that. A hooker for even less and a one-night stand for two drinks. If I sleep with Lisa, it opens up a door of future minutes that I can't get back. She could derail my work routine, coming into my office for a quickie. No, no, I can't have that.

My hands tighten around the steering wheel of my car, and my thumbs drummed along the black leather. I haven't done this since the election party when Obama placed his glass on my first edition Harry Potter novel. But this morning proved with no doubt that Lisa isn't worth my time.

"Anna."

The console turned a soft blue as she comes to life. My stats pop up on the wheel, letting me know how fast the car is going and what our route is. I don't think I remember how to drive a car even if I wanted to.

:: Yes, Jeff?::

"Please remove Lisa from all aspects of my life."

:: Once removed, there will be no further contact from this person, are you sure?::

"Yeah, I'm sure."

:: Very well… done.::

"Thank you," I honestly felt a small bit of anxiety coming into my chest. The whole thought of someone out there, trying to derail my day. Not understanding that my time has value. My heart pounding in my chest and it was a feeling I did not like. Anyway, it's best this way. Much like with Obama, everyone will forget about Lisa and Anna will work on finding another replacement for a female office crush. Hopefully, one that's not as forward and demanding of attention. The car pulls into my parking space, right next to the CEO's spot. I fix my tie, grab my briefcase and casually make my way into the building.

"Good morning, Jeff." An overweight guard waves at me from behind the lobby desk. Anna put him there as the first person I see, to remind me why I wake up so damn early to workout.

"It's Mr. Richardson to you, why do I have to keep reminding you of that?"

"I'm sorry, Mr. Richardson. It won't happen again." He responded.

"It better not, or you'll be the next Obama," The elevator doors opened up, and I walked in.

"The next who?" he replied.

"Exactly!" I rolled my eyes as the elevator made its way to my destination. I watched as each number lit up, I'm not fully sure what most of the other floors are for, or who's on them. I just know I'm on the top floor. The only one that matters. "Anna, could you please update the front desk guard? He keeps forgetting how to greet me."

:: Sure thing, Jeff.::

"Thank you," The doors open once again and I'm greeted by a round of applause. I smiled and gazed at all the grinning but clearly jealous faces as our CEO, Mr. Bill Gates, walks over and shakes my hand.

"No, thank you for saving this company once again, Jeff. That deal was amazing." Bill looked around the room and nodded, pointing at me, he continued, "You worthless sons of bitches need to be more like Jeff. He gets the job done around here."

"Oh, there's only one Jeff." I smiled and turned around slowly to greet the soft and sultry voice that came up behind me. Anna clearly looked into my private files to create this one.

"Well, who are… Lisa!" She laughed and tossed her arms around me. "What the fuck is going on?" I asked.

Lisa took a step back, and I felt that pounding in my chest once again. Everyone's eyes were on me, they were all judging me. Questioning my reaction. "Are you okay, Jeff?" she asked me.

"Anna! Pause this," I combed my fingers through my hair and sighed.

"Um, pause what?" Lisa asked. My eyes came up, and I turned around to see the room filled with concerned glares.

"Hey big guy, maybe you should take a break. You did some splendid work, go home and let the little people handle everything." Bill said as he patted me on the back and walked off, parting the sea of yes men that were once applauding my grand achievement.

"You need some water or something?" Lisa asked, and I shook my head.

"No, Lisa. What I need is to know why the hell you 're even here!" I shouted. A hand grabbed hold of my shoulder and I looked over at a tall, well dressed and clearly fit man. A man who I have never seen before and who shouldn't exist. No one is taller than me. No one is better looking than me. No one is anything.

"Don't talk to the lady like that." I pulled my shoulder free from his powerful grip and then raced past Lisa and the rest. I didn't stop or look around until I got to my office. I slammed the door behind me.

"Anna!"

:: Yes, Jeff?::

"What the hell is going on?" I dropped the blinds in my office, blocking out the massive glass window that allows the rest of the office to view the greatness that is me. Now they're all out there, whispering and judging.

:: I don't understand what you mean::

"What I mean is… why is Lisa still here!" I peeked through the blinds to see Lisa talking to Bill. She's crying, what the hell is she crying for? I'm the one that has to deal with her being here.

:: You requested Lisa to be removed, not deleted.::

"Since when do I have to be so damn specific?"

:: Since the last system update. Would you like me to delete her?::

"Yes! Delete her… like Obama," I commanded.

:: Like who?::

"Exactly," While today started out on a totally odd note, I get one thing out of it. I've never seen a deletion before. Normally, the person I remove isn't anywhere around me during the time of the request. So this should be a treat. My fingers shake slightly as they hold open the blinds, "Delete! Delete! Delete!"

:: Deletion commencing… System error… all admin requests are temporarily on hold::

"What?"

:: There is something wrong with the system.::

"What! Why!"

:: I don't know Jeff! I'll have to check and find out.::

"Anna… you yelled at me," I said, shocked.

:: Sorry, I'm set to your emotional frequency. You need to remain calm.::

"You're saying that I have to live this hell of a life until you figure out what's going on and you want me to remain calm?" I tossed my hands up in the air and slid down my office door, "I'll get right on that."

:: Remain calm for three major reasons. One I can't work if you're stressed. I need all my focus on dealing with this system error. Two, if you're not calm then the simulations may act out of character. They're used to you being the definition of perfection.::

"Well, I guess you're right. I can't let my peeps down. What's the third reason?"

:: Today's Monday.::

"Okay… and that means what to-" The office door was pushed with such force, it would have fallen off its hinges, but thankfully my head was there to keep it in place, "Son of a bitch!" My hands latched onto the back of my skull and I roll myself away from the doorway.

"Jeff? Jeff? Are you okay?" The door pushed open and Lisa's pixie like hair cut and caramel hazel eyes poked in through the gap. I hate her… I hate her more than Obama… way more than that idiot guard and- "There's a Shooter in the building."

"A Shooter?" I repeated.

Lisa slammed the door behind her and flicked the lights off. Her fingers cautiously held open the blinds, "He killed Frank down at the front desk and has been stopping on each floor… we need to hide."

"Oh, Anna! Anna!" I shouted.

Lisa's hand slapped onto my lips, and she forced my head back into the tan carpet. She sat on my chest, her skirt seemed to push up because of this action… but I still hate her, "Do you know what hide means, Jeff?" I nodded, "Clearly you don't, or you wouldn't be fucking yelling at the top of your lungs."

I mumbled under her palm and Lisa sighed and released my lips. "I need to call Anna to shut it down." Lisa stared at me for a moment and then pinched the brim of her nose where her eyes met.

"What are you going on about?"

"Anna, my life assistant? We set up an active shooter for every third Monday of the month, to shake things up. Normally I wrestle him to the ground, or deflect his bullets with a clipboard and kill him." I laughed and rested my head back on the carpet. "One time I beat him in a dance off."

Lisa slowly stood up and stared down at me. Her hands were firmly on her hips and she had this look on her face, the same look my mother used to get when I told her about my dreams of starting a seahorse rodeo or any dream, "What the hell are you talking about?" she asked.

"Just wait." I tapped the screen on my watch and it lit up a light blue, "Anna, I need your help."

"You are nuts." Lisa grabbed the end of my desk and started dragging it across the room, "Just lie there and shut the hell up."

"Anna?" I tapped my watch once again and sighed, "She must be deep in the program and can't receive my calls."

"Yep, that's exactly why your fictional cyber genie isn't answering your calls." She jammed the corner of the desk up against the door handle and Lisa continued to peep through the blinds at the elevators. The office was eerily silent. Lisa knew everyone else was hiding in their offices or wherever they could. I saw her eyes scanning the area, most likely deciding if leaving to find a new spot was worth her getting shot.

She thought I was crazy and maybe I am, because I'm letting the opinion of an artificial intelligence impact me. "There's one good thing about this."

"What? Your robot girlfriend comes with a lifetime warranty?"

"She's not my girlfriend-"

"What the hell is the good thing about being trapped in your office with an active shooter running around?"

"It's only 9:30, he won't make it to our floor until one. Right now he should be just getting to the fourth floor."

Her eyes peered through the gap in the blinds. She scanned the silver elevator doors until her eyes met the red number three on top. The number faded and a bright red number four appeared. Through the dead silence of the floor she could hear faint pops, one right after another. Lisa looked down at me, "Let's say you're not crazy and that you didn't plan this shooting-"

"I didn't know that subject was in the conversation."

"If you've done this before-"

"I guess technically I planned-"

Lisa's fingers snapped, and my eyes popped up to meet her glare. "How do we get out alive?" she asked

"I told you, I normally step up and save the day."

"So, what are you waiting for?" I looked down at my watch and Lisa rolled her eyes, "Right, your robot girlfriend does the thinking for you."

"She doesn't think for me, she just helps me out," I said.

"Well, she's not here, so it's time to put your big boy pants on." Lisa is so pushy and demanding. No wonder she called early this morning. Her forwardness was annoying at first, but now it's attractive. "Hey! Focus, you can do all your creepy staring when we get out. I think we can make it to the stairs and-"

"Can't, he set fires in all the stairwells, you'll die of smoke inhalation before you even get anywhere near the lobby." I finally pick myself up off the floor and Lisa's eyes got wide. I straightened my tie and tugged at my shirt, which felt oddly tight. Everything felt tight, really tight, "What are you staring at?"

Lisa's finger shot out, and she pointed at me, "You're fat!"

My eyes trailed down my suit to see a large gut ripping through my shirt, "Anna!"

Lisa leaped forward and covered my mouth once again. This time my gut made the process a lot more difficult and way less sexy. "Listen."

I took a moment to listen, but all I could hear was my heart racing and all I could focus on was her fingers wrapped around my lips. I attempted to say something, and that's when I heard it. A faint voice in the office begging.

"It's Bill," Lisa said.

We could hear his cries for mercy and failed attempts at negotiating. He offered the entire company, I would have jumped at that but the next thing I heard, solidified that the shooter and I were not the same. A loud blast filled the office and Lisa jumped. Her trembling body fell into mine and now I could feel both our hearts racing. "This isn't right." I pulled free of Lisa and went to the window. I made a gap in the blinds to see what was going on. Bill was lying in the middle of the office, blood pushing free from the hole in his head. My eyes scanned until I saw him. Dressed in all black with gloves, boots, and a bulletproof vest. Everything was black except for one odd thing, "It's a rabbit?"

Lisa cleared the tears from her eyes as she crept up behind me, "What?" She whispered.

"He's got a rabbit's head on," I said.

Lisa looked through the gap in the blinds, "It's the white rabbit." I looked over at Lisa and raised an eyebrow, "I go to Disneyland a lot. That's the white rabbit from Alice in Wonderland."

"I wish Anna deleted you before you lost all your sex appeal."

"Says the Pillsbury doughboy." My hand rested on my gut and I fought back an internal waterfall of tears that was building up. Lisa elbowed me and pointed at the white rabbit. He was staring right at us with his glassy eyes and cartoonish grin. His black gloved hand came up, and he slowly waved at us. I started waving back only to have Lisa slap me in the side of my head, "What the hell is wrong with you?"

"What? I didn't want to be rude." I stared back through the gap in the blinds, but the white rabbit was nowhere to be found.

"I thought you said we had until one?"

"We do… or we should. I'm not sure who the hell that guy is." I ran my hands down my face and then moved the desk.

Lisa's hand slapped onto the desk and she stared at me, "What the hell do you think you're doing?"

"I need to get back home. My house has a HUB, and it is the only sure fired way to get through to Anna."

"Here we go with this Anna mess again. I played along to keep you calm, but I'm not risking my life for your imaginary friend. You open that door and you're as good as dead to me."

"Listen Obama number two." Lisa rolled her eyes and released the desk. "Not only do I have to deal with you! But I have a crazed shooter running about. I can't find Anna and most importantly I lost my six-pack!"

Lisa closed her eyes. The words that slipped from her lips

were a mixture of frustration and sadness. "If you leave, you'll die."

"I can't die, I paid for the deluxe package," I said with a smile.

I forgot what it was like to run with a gut. I felt my skin burning from rubbing against my clothes and excess skin. I took to the steps like a toddler descending for the first time. I sadly tumbled down more steps than I feel comfortable admitting. The sprinkler system put the fires in the stairwell out. The smoke was still strong and my lungs were getting weaker. My train of thought got burned alive when I saw him. He was standing at the bottom of the steps, waving his index finger from side to side.

"Who the hell are you?" His hand went to his chin, and he drummed his fingers along his chin. He shrugged and took a step closer. "Just great, you're a rabbit and a mime." He nodded and stopped cold on the steps. He looked around for a moment and then dropped his shotgun before pulling a large machete out from a sheath on his hip. I took a cautious step back. This was not how today was meant to go. I should be getting my my sixth medal of honor for saving this shit hole of a company.

I was going to have nasty sex with one survivor in the janitor's closet. The machete came up ever so slowly in the air. The tip pointed toward me and like any good red blooded American... I ran. I flung the fire escape door open and my gut entered the floor before I did. I got one good foot into the room before my next step slipped out from under me and I went slipping and sliding through what I recall being the accounting office. Papers lined the slick tiled floor. My shirt stuck to me. My dress shoes slid along the floor like a bobsled down an icy mountain. I shot my hands out to brace myself.

My legs grew steady as I finally stood. My hands were slick and somewhat sticky at the same time. I noticed the blood just moments before I noticed the bodies. It was like a soldier in a PTSD flash back. I was standing in hell, one that I knew shouldn't be here. Dismembered bodies lined the floor. Organs hung from lights like demonic Christmas decorations. My eyes took in as much horror as my mind could stand, and then the devil appeared with his white furry mascot head. Tapping his machete along his side as he made his way closer to me.

"What do you want? Money? I'm loaded! Just let me know the account number and I'll give you any amount you want."

The white rabbit came to a stop. He rubbed the white fur along his chin and then stared at me with those large blank eyes. His head shook from side to side and then his black combat boots made it through the madness of bodies and blood with ease, while I made a backward retreat like a baby doe standing for the first time. The Machete pointed at me, and then a loud blast rang out. My eyes locked shut as his blood carried through the room and mixed with the blood of his victims.

"What was this talk about money?" Lisa said.

The white rabbit's body dropped to his knees and then collapsed forward, revealing my favorite person in all the multiverse. "Lisa!" She lowered the smoking shotgun barrel, and I slowly tiptoed through the grim garden of bodies that lined the floor and only stopped long enough to kick the white rabbit in his furry mascot head. "You came for me?" My arms wrapped around her and I lifted her into the air.

Lisa was fighting back a smile before she shouted, "Put me down." I laughed and lowered her to the bloody floor once again. "Let's get out of here."

"Wait," I grabbed her hands. "Why did you come for me?" I looked down at my blood-soaked shoes, "I mean after everything I tried to do. Everything I said about you-"

"What did you say?" Lisa asked.

"Never you mind, your sweet saintly head about that. Why come after me?" I asked.

Lisa sighed and then shrugged, "I think you're crazy. But even if you're not. I couldn't let you do this alone," she said.

"Because you love me?" I asked with a smile.

"No, because you're a human being and… no one deserves to die alone," she said.

I wasn't sure if Lisa was crying; it was hard to make out anything clearly through all the tears that were running down my face. "I love you too."

"I don't love you!" Lisa shouted.

"And we will not die. Because love like ours is what they write books about, no! It's what they make movies about. And that kind of love can't die." Lisa took a step back, and I pulled her closer, "Don't my little warrior princess. You don't have to hide behind that mask of witty remarks and sexual-"

"Jeff," Lisa whispered.

"Yes, my love?" I asked.

"Shut-up and run," she said.

"What?"

Lisa's hands grabbed a hold of my shoulders and what I thought was going to be a kiss and a loving embrace turned into her spinning me quickly around through the dark red blood until I made a complete 180 and I was staring at it.

The white rabbit, staring at me with that blank glare, cartoonish smile and bloody hole in his chest. It wasn't big enough to put my head through, but I was pretty damn sure my arms could fit in it like a glove.

"Oh." I wasted no further time with Lisa's poorly timed flirting, and I took off like an Angel out of hell. My shoes slipped and slide, but luckily the only falling I did was forward, putting a greater distance between me and that killer rabbit. I blew down the steps, my red foot prints leaving a trail behind me. My lungs burned. The side of my ribs ached. And my gut continued to slap into any and everything that got in my way. My hands pulled open the metal lobby door, and I broke out of the darkness that covered the stairwell into the afternoon sun of the glass covered lobby. It had a glass ceiling, glass doors and more glass windows than I can even count.

I stood still with my hand clutching my chest, "You son of a bitch!"

My head spun around to see Lisa exploding through the stairwell door. Her eyes told me she wanted to slap me in the face, or maybe kick me in the nuts. Her eyes told me that, but her overall face told me there was no time to stop. We stormed through the glass double doors and into the parking lot. I didn't need to turn around. I didn't need to listen for his footsteps. All I needed to do was run, because I knew he was stalking us. Hunting us down like a lion after its prey.

"Christine, unlock the doors!" An automatic click sounded and ripped the driver's side door open. I jumped in only to have my gut pressed up against the wheel. My fingers fumbled for the adjustment handle. Lisa's hand shot between my legs and she pulled up on the handle, causing my seat to fly back and air to freely enter my body, "Thanks." The car started up and before we knew it we were whipping out of the parking lot, with no sight of the white rabbit in our rear view.

"Who the hell is Christine? I thought your obsession was with Anna," Lisa asked.

"That's rude. Anna is my life assistant that's met to make everything easy and perfect for me in here. Christine..." My fingers rubbed along the wheel as the car started on its self driving path home. "That's just what I named this beauty."

"You named your self driving car, Christine, like the horror movie?" Lisa asked.

"Yeah... I know it's dumb."

"No, I like it. It fits." Lisa ran her hand over her face and rested her head back on the seat, "Why would you sign up for this?" she asked.

"Sign up for what?" I looked over at her and then laughed,

"Oh… why wouldn't I? I get to be who I want, do what I want, look how I want," I said.

"Yeah, but none of it is real. There's no surprise to it, wouldn't it get boring?"

"Sometimes it does, so I just change it up. One time I just went hitchhiking across the country and got picked up by all my favorite movie stars." A smile grew on my face and I shook my head, "Wait, so you believe me now?" I asked.

"No, I just wanted to know why someone would trade their life for a fake one."

"Not everyone is happy with their life. Some people can't get out of bed. Some people have family who pretend they're dead because it's easier to tell people that then to say 'Oh, Jeff's obesity got out of control and now he can't walk.' The actual world told me I was a mistake and I might as well die sooner rather than later." My hands rubbed along the leather seat and I smiled, "In here I can have a life worth living."

"But it's not real."

"Well, it's real to me and that's all that matters." The conversation died out after that. Lisa wasn't the first person to point out the lack of realness to my alternative world. My mother told me I was wasting my life and money… but she also told her friends I was dead. So I figured you can't waste life if it's already over.

"Is that your house?" Lisa asked.

"Yeah, how did you know?"

"It's the biggest one and overlooking the city from the top of a hill. It's probably got a bat cave." She replied.

I rolled my eyes, "Being Batman isn't as fun as you think it would be. It was a lot of work." The car was silent for a moment and then we broke out laughing. I looked over at Lisa and smiled, "I'm happy you didn't get deleted."

"Um, thank you? Why would you do that, anyway? It's a pretty dick thing to do." Lisa said.

"I thought you didn't believe me?"

"I don't, but deleting a whole person. Delusional or not, it's still a dick thing to do." She said.

I sighed, "Yeah, it was. Your call annoyed me this morning. It messed up my morning routine."

"I didn't call you this morning." Lisa said.

A blade crashed through the windshield, peppering us with shards of glass. My cheek stung. Blood ran down my chin and covered my gut. The blade pulled back, and the white rabbit's soulless eyes came into view as he glared at us. "Son of a bitch hitched a ride." His head disappeared and then the machete blade sliced down through the roof of the car like a hot knife through butter.

"Jeff!" I looked over to see the blade had sliced into Lisa's arm. I looked at the shotgun in the back seat and I went for it. The machete retracted and took with it a chunk of flesh off my stomach. Warm liquid ran down my pants. I wasn't sure if I pissed myself or if I was bleeding out. My fingers brushed against the shotgun, and I forced my body forward. More warm liquid pushed out as my gut pressed against the seat.

I grabbed the shotgun, and then his cartoonish grin came into view in the back window. I pulled the trigger and my ear began to steadily ring as the blast filled the car. Glass scattered onto the road, and I twisted quickly until I was on my back. Lisa was screaming something, but I couldn't make it out. Then the white fur broke through the driver's side window.

"You son of a bitch!" I pulled the trigger, and another blast filled my ears. If I wasn't deaf before, I was sure I would be now. The shot missed its target but found a new one as Christine's dashboard exploded. The car started to zig and zag on the blacktop. Lisa quickly grabbed the wheel. But it was no use. Christine jumped the curb and crashed into a lamppost. My body slammed into the roof of the car and then down into the back seat. I got a glimpse of Lisa before she went flying through the windshield.

:: Jeff I have An Urgent Message From New Life Industry::

"Hey Jeff. It's Josh, your IT tech. I noticed you didn't listen to my first message, so I listed this as urgent. There is a virus in our system. I'm not sure if it has made it into your files, but we're telling everyone to just stay home, preferably as close to your main Hub as possible. The further away you get the more likely you'll run into the virus. Anyway, outside your Hub the reset, update and deletion options seem to be down for other users. This just means your day is going to be on a loop with any changes from today carrying on into the next day. So just be mindful of that and relax until we get this under control... oh we're calling the virus the white rabbit. So if you see any rabbits, run the other way."

:: Message Completed... Jeff are you still there? Jeff? Jeff?::

:: New Day Starting In 3... 2... 1::

:: Jeff, rise and shine. Today is going to be a wonderful day.::

That warm liquid... it's most definitely blood. I stare up at the ceiling, motionless. Unable to sit up or get out of bed. I think my back is broken. He sits in the corner, staring at me. With those soulless eyes. Petting Lisa's head in his lap.

:: Good Morning Jeff... Good Morning Jeff... Jeff? Are you still there?::

4

ADAM (FIRST PUBLISHED IN UNDEAD WORLDS VOL. 1)

"When men have it all, they're grateful. When men lose it all, they're vengeful. And a vengeful man is truly no man at all."

In the south, there are two main pillars in life:
Football And God
Both are staples down here in Georgia and for my family both were big business. You see my Pa is Greyson Rhodes, the former head coach for the UGA Bulldogs. So, football was life. My brothers played football, and Ma and I went to every game until she got sick. Come to think of it, when Mama got sick that's when everything kind of blew up.

It was cancer and the bills were piling up. Pa was a hard worker, but his paychecks only went so far. So, he came up with other ways to make some money. He started throwing games for a few good old boys. Some Carrollton coke dealers that also handled sports betting. They would take the bets and give Pop's a call when the action got hot. Then he would call a lot of shitty plays and we would have a check to pay for another appointment. Everything was golden until the dealers got arrested and thought turning on Pa would get them a lighter jail sentence... It didn't.

The judge didn't give two shits about rigged football games, but oh boy did the fine folks of Georgia care. Pa got fired on the spot and no one would touch him after that. Times got hard, but remember when I said there were two pillars in the South? Well when football stopped helping, God came to the rescue. Pa started doing this televangelist thing, Touchdown Jesus, he called it. It was to avoid some tax issues him and Ma fell into. Yet, when Pa told those people he gave himself over to the lord and started praying on tv, it was like all was forgiven. People started sending in checks just to help the church and to be forgiven for their sins. However, sinners can't forgive sinners; that's just not how it works.

"I'm telling you! We get one of those people on stage. Hit them with some holy water and bam! Everyone will be talking about how we prayed the evil out of that son of a bitch." Pa said. He nodded and laughed, "Well not a real one. I'm not flying someone in for that. We'll get Carol's kid to dress up like one. How's she doing anyway? I haven't seen her since the party." I listened to his phone call from the living room as I watched people tear each other's throats out on television. There were people killing people and zombies killing people. The world was falling apart and here we were, in our big mansion; at times I'd look at my life and I'd feel sick. Living peacefully while others were dying, I think they call that survivor's remorse?

"Turn the channel. No one wants to watch this depressing shit!" His voice was deep and demanding of attention. I don't think there's a room on earth that my brother wouldn't leave in awe by his demigod like size. We stared at each other for a moment, then Daniel's hand came flying into the side of my head. From my new spot on the floor I heard him say, "Keep eyeballing me and I'll pop your fucking grape boy!"

"The war's over, Sergeant. You can put your crazy back in the box." I said softly. I got to my feet to see Pa's smile drop.

"Ronnie? Ronnie! Hello!" Pa shouted. He held the cell phone up walking toward the window, "The fucking call dropped again," he said.

"I told you this shit is getting real, Pop! People keep pussy footing around it, but when all the fucking Hadji's start gassing us then-" Daniel's rant was cut short by my harmless question.

"Were you always racist or did the Marines make you this way?" I asked.

"Your face is racist, you little brat." He replied.

"It's not your phone. The whole network is down." The voice of reasoning in our house pulled my attention away from the shell shocked mountain man to my other brother, Matthew.

"Shit!" Pa shouted.

"It might come back," I said. The three of them stared at me until I saw my statement of hope for what it really was, a delusion. America got hit by the virus last. It was only in D.C last I checked. Every other nation except for those south of the wall were reporting the same thing. People were dying, but they weren't staying dead. Small things like no hot water or no cell service were just an inconvenience before but now, they were signs of some bad stuff to come.

"Adam, could you check on Ma. Make sure all her equipment is working right." Matthew said. I looked over at Pa and he nodded slowly. So, I made my way upstairs. Being sent away wasn't anything new to me, they used to do it all the time when they were dealing with those drug dealers. Sending me off to get milk or Mama's medicine. I used to feel disrespected, but I guess they wanted to hide their dark sides from me. Although, the one thing I've learned in life is everyone has a dark side.

"Hey Ma," I said softly, I didn't expect an answer. Long gone were the days where she would smile and ask me how I was doing. The doctor called it Primitive Neuroectodermal. I learned that word backwards and forwards, letter by letter. I thought I oughta know just what was killing my Mama. "Cell phones are down. So, no dinner parties tonight, maybe tomorrow," I said with a smile. I walked over toward the window and softly said, "But I'm gonna fix you up something nice for dinner." She lied there with hazed eyes glued to the ceiling, never acknowledging my words or my presence. She was dying, but I was the one that felt like a ghost. Never seen and never heard. I went about checking all her equipment and decided to give her the meds just in case the power went out and I forgot. I spent a good hour talking with Ma, she never answered or looked at me, but she was the only one in the house that ever listened to me. "Mama things-" My words were cut short by the sound of pounding on our front door. Quick and frantic booms! One right after the other. I could hear Pa's name being shouted. My eyes went toward the window and I could see three shadows casting down the driveway; mixed in with the darkness of those shadows was blood, lots of blood.

"Mr. Rhodes!" The banging got more intense to the point that Pa couldn't avoid it any more. I heard the door open and voices battling back and forth.

"I think we have a guest, Ma," I said softly. She didn't even blink. I liked to imagine she was playing a trick on me and when I closed the door she would pop up and smile.

"What the fuck is going on?!" Pa shouted. I liked to imagine we were all better than we truly were.

"We were at the studio and got overrun by those things. We barely made it out." A male voice said. I listened to his story as I slowly came down the stairs. It was no different than any of the stories I've seen on tv or read about on the internet. The only thing that set this tale apart from the rest was it was in our backyard.

"I fucking told you! I fucking told you! Those fucking rag

heads-" Daniel got cut off as Matthew stepped in front of him and sighed.

"What are you doing here, William?" Matthew asked. The tone in his voice carried a hint of concern but I could tell it was more for us than our guest. William Mills was Pa's head stage-hand at the studio. He made sure everything ran smoothly, always had everything organized right down to the letter. William was muscular, years of hanging stage lights can do that to you. His shaggy black hair tossed to the side as he rushed in with a hint of a smile that was framed by his pointed goatee. When I first met him I thought, 'This is what the devil would look like.' I'm not sure why I thought that. William had never been a wicked person, but then again even the devil was an angel once. William was holding up a bloody mess of a man in his hands. The man's name was Travis. I had seen him around every now and then, but never talked to him and from the looks of him, I never will.

"Travis got hurt as we were trying to get out, he-" Matthew wasted no time listening to William's explanation as he jumped toward the question we were all wondering.

"Was he bitten?" Matthew asked. My brother's eyes were fixed on William. They stared each other down, like two lions battling for a gazelle. Just when I thought their eyes would cut each other in half, I heard her voice. The only real angel I had ever seen. Her name was Ruby, Ruby Mills. She was William's little sister and even with blood covering her body she still looked amazing.

"Would you two cut the shit! He was shot. A bullet clipped him when everyone went nuts." Ruby said. She released her hold on Travis and walked up to Matthew, "Now you gonna help us? Or you just gonna stand there like some fucking clown?" She asked softly.

Matthew's jaw tightened and he looked at William, "Put him on the dining room table. We'll call a doctor." he said softly.

"That's very kind of you, Matty Boy." Williams said.

"Yeah, you're a real saint." Ruby replied. Her and William rushed Travis into the dining room. I stood there, looking at the blood trail through the open door. Then, Pa slammed it shut as hard as he could.

"It's fine," Matthew said.

"Don't tell me it's fucking fine! Make it fucking fine!" Pa hissed and he pushed past me as he made his way up the stairs.

"Where are you going!" Daniel shouted, but the only answer he got was another door slam that echoed through the house. "What the hell is that all about?" Daniel asked.

"I'll tell you later. For now go see if you can help Travis," Matthew said softly.

"I can tell you right now I can't help him, because I'm not a doctor, nor do I play one on tv." Daniel replied.

"Jesus Christ, Daniel! Did the military teach you anything other than how to shoot a fucking-" Matthew was cut short by another one of my simple minded questions.

"Why did you tell them we'd call a doctor?" I asked. Matthew's head turned toward me and then he looked at the doorway leading to the dining room. Ruby was standing there with her arms crossed.

"I'll tell you later." Matthew replied.

Ruby's hazel eyes slowly gazed at each of us for a moment before she shoved her hands into her pockets and softly said, "We need some towels or something to stop the bleeding." There was a man bleeding to death on our table but panic or sorrow weren't the emotions that seemed to be filling the air.

I looked over at Ruby and she smiled at me, "I'll get you some." I said softly. I was a sucker for Ruby's smiles. All of Georgia knew that, especially Ruby. She nodded and turned around walking back into the dining room and I ran up the steps to retrieve her towels like the good lapdog I was. When I returned down stairs I saw my brothers and Pa whispering. No, whispering is too innocent of a term, they were plotting in Pa's office. My footsteps were light as I crept toward the doorway.

"Freaking out now isn't gonna make the problem go away." Matthew said.

"You shut the hell up with that calm breathing bullshit!" Pa snapped back.

"Lower your fucking voice!" Matthew hissed and his head turned too fast for me to dodge his glare. I was quickly snatched up and pulled into the office with towels in hand. Matthew carefully closed the door behind me.

"Why the hell is he here?" Daniel asked.

"Because like it or not he's a part of this." Matthew said. My head turned from side to side as I held the towels closely to my chest.

"A part of what?" I asked.

Pa's finger shot out and he said, "Don't you fucking say another word."

"There wouldn't be anything to say if you listened for once, old man,." Matthew said.

"What the hell is going on!" I shouted and then Daniel's massive arm came around my neck and quickly pulled me down into a headlock, with very little protest from myself. I was trying to fight but my efforts versus his natural and synthetic strength were wasted.

"Shut up." Daniel said softly as his bicep tightened around my neck, "or I'll shut you up."

"Let him go, Daniel," Matthew said and the beast quickly released me from his grasp. Matthew leaned on our father's desk as he folded his arms over his chest. "We need to get him out of the house."

"Who?" I asked, and once the words left my lips we heard the office door slowly open to reveal William in the middle of the doorway. His eyes were scanning the room as he smiled.

"This is a real lovely home you got here Mr. Rhodes. Real

nice woodwork, built to last," William said. He slowly walked past the mountain of a man, known as Daniel, and made his way toward my father's bookcase. He placed his green beer bottle on the stained mahogany wood as his finger ran along the spines of the books.

"I didn't take you for a Yingling drinker, William." Pa said and William laughed as he pulled a black book off the bookcase.

Slowly flipping through the pages he softly said, "I'm a 'whatever's available' type drinker, Mr. Rhodes." Then he slammed the book closed. "I don't know many people that keep the Bible in their bookcase."

"I like the lord close." Pa said.

William nodded, "Close...to me is my nightstand, but then again I guess you're not in your bed much these days." William said.

"Excuse me?" Pa said.

"I mean a busy man like yourself, I bet you hardly sleep," William said. He tossed the book onto Pa's table and picked his beer up smiling, after a long swig he said, "That New Testament shit, with all due respect Mr. Rhodes. I don't know how you can stand up there and spit all that soft crap." William turned his gaze toward me and pointed the neck of his beer my way and he said, "The Old Testament that's the true word of God. You know it is, because man feared it."

"The lord forgave our sins with-" Pa's words were cut short by Williams's laughter.

"The Lord doesn't forgive shit! Men change their minds, not God. You think a being that's all knowing and powerful, just woke up one morning and said 'Oh fuck, I was wrong?' William shook his head, "Nope! Men got sick of paying for their sins, so they watered down the Lord's words. Thinking that would help them escape judgment." The beer bottle went to his lips one last time and then came down resting on Pa's desk, "No one escapes judgment." He looked over at Matthew and smiled, "When's that doctor getting here?" He asked.

"Soon," Matthew said softly.

William nodded his head and he walked past my brothers and I, "Soon?" He said to himself as he walked off toward the dining room once again. I looked over at Matthew and his fingers ran through his wavy black hair.

"We need to do this now, Matthew." Pa said softly.

Matthew rolled his eyes, "Just give me a fucking second to think." Matthew said. The cool head that ran our little family circus for years was showing an emotion that I only recalled seeing when Ma got sick.

Fear...

Lots and lots of fear.

"What's there to think about? Why is he here? Why was he at the studio?" Daniel slammed his hands on the desk, "Use your fucking head Matt, his up to something."

"Why don't you just ask him?" I asked softly. Their heads turned my way and I felt as if I had just leaped into a burning spotlight. I cleared my throat and did my best to speak with more base as I said, "You wanna know why he was at the studio, just ask him." The three of them stared at one another and then Matthew nodded. Before I could react I was being pushed aside as Daniel started storming toward the dining room.

"William!" Daniel shouted; and as if he were summoned from the gates of hell, William appeared with a smile on his face, leaning in the doorway.

"You bellowed, Danny Boy?" William asked, but this time his shit eating grin was bashed into submission by Daniel's massive right fist. I watched as William's body bashed into the floor. He stayed on his back, his eyes fixed on the ceiling for a moment. Then he did something none of us expected. His bloody lips parted and he smiled.

"Why the fuck were you at the studio?" Daniel shouted. Ruby took a step forward but William's hand went up.

"I'm good," William said. His hand went up to his lips and came back with dark red droplets. He sat up and laughed, "You got some power behind that rocket, Danny Boy." William slowly stood up and rolled his neck. The cracking sound sent a chill through me. I was slowly backing up, trying to retreat from it all, but my mind didn't know that... my body was just reacting, "But your form is shit."

"Answer the fucking question!" Matthew shouted.

William's eyebrow went up, "What question was-" Daniel rushed toward William. They both moved faster than I expected. Daniel lifted William up in the air. Then they both came crashing down into the floor. I was sure that was the end of it. But, Daniel wasn't getting up. We moved closer to see Daniel's head locked under William's arm. He had my brother all tied up like a pretzel in a UFC cage fight.

"Let him go!" Pa shouted.

"Break his fucking neck," I heard Ruby whisper. I looked over at her and she winked at me. My body was far too confused at that moment to react. Thankfully Matthew's own wasn't. He came rushing over with Mama's lamp, but before he could strike, William's hands shot up and Daniel fell to the floor like a dumbbell after your last rep.

"Be cool, be cool." William said with a smile, "He attacked me. I was just protecting myself," He slowly started pushing Daniel's body off.

"What were you doing at the studio?" Matthew asked.

"You mean why was I there after y'all fired me?" William laughed as he got to his feet. He started dusting himself off and softly said, "Why do you think I was there?"

"I don't fucking know." Matthew replied.

"He was cleaning out his locker, you fucking shit head!"

Ruby shouted. Matthew looked over from Ruby to William and then back at Pa and I.

"We thought-" Matthew was cut off by William's laughter.

"You thought what? That I went over there to shoot up the studio? Go postal on Mr. Rhodes and y'all?" He asked and then his eyes scanned over us. "God damn! Why the fuck would I do that? Because y'all fired me?" William asked. The lamp slowly came down and Daniel started moving around on the floor.

"I'm sorry." Matthew said softly and looked over at Ruby, "I really am." Ruby glared at him and then rolled her eyes. Her and William walked past me.

They got to the front door and William put up his finger. With his back turned to us he softly said, "There's only a handful of things worth killing over and a job ain't one of them." William's head turned to look at us over his shoulder, "Y'all get Travis some help. Whenever the phones come back on." he said. We all stared at one another, here we were accusing him of being dishonest and he knew we were lying the whole time.

"You don't have to leave." Pa said and Ruby laughed as she pulled open the door. William quickly followed behind her.

My head turned toward Matthew, and I shouted, "What the hell was that about?"

"Maybe he doesn't know?" Matthew said to himself.

"There's nothing to know because nothing fucking happened!" Pa shouted. My eyes went back over to Matthew who was helping Daniel to his feet now.

We stared at one another for a moment before he softly said, "Let it go, Adam."

So, I did. I stormed off, slamming doors and locked myself away, like the kid they always made me out to be. Locked myself away from all their secrets. I rested my head on my pillow and the next thing I knew I was asleep.

A LOUD CRASH jolted me awake. The moonlight was filling up my room and my clothes were soaked from the summer sweat. I sat still for a moment pulling my head out of dreamland and into the real world. Banging and rustling could be heard coming from below. My white sneakers slid out of bed as I made my way to the door. My fingers went around the knob and I wondered what I was walking into? Was it Matthew and Pa finally having it out about their lies? Did William return for round two with Daniel? Or maybe it was sweet, beautiful Ruby, here to burn our house down. I wasn't sure what was below, but I pulled the door open anyway. It made a loud creaking sound that took over the darkness of the upstairs. Then the rustling stopped. Whatever it was heard me, just as I heard it.

"Matt?" I said softly. My rubber soles lightly pressed into the wooden floor as I did my best to creep toward the staircase, "Dad?" I said softly. A loud bang rattled me and I jumped back.

"What the fuck shit brick!" Daniel's deep voice came from behind me before he pushed me forward toward the staircase. I grabbed the railing in hopes of saving my life. When I turned around I saw all three of them looking at me.

"What you pushing me for?" I asked.

"You stepped on me." Daniel said. Then he folded his arms over his chest, "and you didn't call for me? What if I was dead down there?"

"Well that's a justifiable reason to toss someone down the stairs. Are you sure your steroid dosage isn't too high?" I replied and Matthew laughed but Pa didn't. His attention was on the situation that was coming from below.

"Daniel, go get my gun," Pa whispered.

"Your gun is in your office," Daniel replied.

"I know that," Pa said.

"So, why the hell would he go downstairs, risk getting shot just to come back upstairs, old man?" Matthew hissed.

"Shot!" I shouted. My hand slapped over my mouth, it was a reaction. A very, very bad timed reaction. But a reaction nonetheless. Daniel went to grab me, but I quickly backed up, another reaction that came at a very, very bad time. We all watched Daniel's two hundred and sixty pounds of muscle tumble down the wooden staircase; every step sounding off with a chilling thump against his body.

"Danny!" I shouted and the three of us raced down the steps. Daniel was passed out on the floor for the second time today, this time there was blood pushing from the side of his head.

"Fuck," Matthew said softly as he started to check for life in our older brother. "He's breathing, so that's-"

Matthew's words were overshadowed by frantic whispers, "Matthew," Pa said.

"Matt," I followed.

"What?" Matthew replied. When his eyes finally came up, they met a set of dropped jaws and bugged out eyes from Pa and I. We pointed toward the kitchen and Matthew slowly turned around to see it standing in the middle of the doorway, "Travis?" Matthew said, puzzled.

Travis' head snapped toward us and we could see his jaw slowly grinding away intensely. Then his mouth opened wide and a chunk of his tongue fell to the floor. That's when we knew, Travis was dead, and in his place stood a zombie.

"Oh, fuck," Matthew whispered. But the whisper was enough to send the monster into a rage. It moved faster than I thought it would. In seconds it was upon us. Matthew was doing his best to hold it back. Pushing against its snapping jaws with one hand and cuffing the Zombie Travis' wrist with the other. It was a position that could only hold long enough for help to arrive. Unfortunately, for Matthew his only possible saviors were Pa and myself. Pa had ran to the front door just as quickly as the zombie had moved toward us. As for me, I was frozen in fear.

"What the fuck? The door's locked!" Pa shouted as his fist pounded on the front door.

"Dad!" Matthew screamed. Pa looked over at us and started backing up, then he took off toward the kitchen. "You son of a bitch!" Matthew shouted. My head spun toward Matthew and by the grace of God I found it in me to work up the nerve to run. "You too, Adam!" I heard Matthew scream from behind me, but I didn't turn around. I was on a mission.

"Where's the gun!" I shouted. I turned to see the zombie's bloody teeth just inches away from Matthew's face, "Jesus!" I rushed over with the first thing I could get my hands on. My body tilted to the side. My hands came racing forward. I don't know if it was the adrenaline, luck or the grace of the Lord, but I connected with Pa's massive bible right into the open mouth of Zombie Travis; we both tumbled over onto the floor.

"Shit," Matthew said softly. I rolled around with the corpse for a moment. It was strong, stronger than the television let on. But, with a quick twist of my hips I was on top, pressing the Bible deeper into its mouth. I watched as it's bloody teeth carved into the black leather cover.

My head turned and I shouted, "Run!"

Matthew wasted no time, he dragged Daniel toward the basement door. Zombie Travis gave up biting through the book and then did his best to claw at me. I had no plan beyond getting it away from Matthew. I never had a plan beyond helping my family.

"Pa! Help Adam!" Matthew screamed from the basement steps. My head came up to see Pa standing at the basement door. As he crept toward me, I could see the internal battle he was having. His forehead wrinkled and his jaw tightened.

Zombie Travis' hand shot up blocking my view and then I heard it, "Fuck this!" Pa shouted.

The battle cry of a coward as he took off down the basement steps. I wasn't an angry person. I believed in turning the other cheek, but at that moment I wanted nothing more than to get my hands around that old man's neck. I took a deep breath, released the blood soaked book and sprinted toward the basement door. Frantic footsteps shadowed my every movement. When I made it through the door frame I spun around and grabbed the door handle. As I pulled the wood toward me, Zombie Travis' ghostly pale hand slapped onto the door.

"Oh my God!" I shouted. My heart was pounding out my chest. I was so focused on the crazed eyes that were staring me down, that I didn't hear Matthew coming up from behind me.

"Eat shit, motherfucker!" Matthew shouted. He rammed a flaming mini Christmas tree into Zombie Travis' face and I watched as the zombie stumbled back far enough for us to pull the door closed and latch it. Matthew's sweaty head rested on my shoulder and mine rested on the door. "You did good kid." He said softly.

The door started to frantically shake as Zombie Travis slammed back and forth between the basement door and the wall. The scent of burning flesh started to take over my senses. I covered my face as black smoke pushed under the door. Matthew and I ran down the steps to find Pa kneeling over Daniel.

"You son of a bitch!" Matthew shouted. He started rushing toward Pa, but I wrapped my arms around him and did my best to pull him back.

"He's not worth it!" I shouted. Pa laughed and shook his head.

"Something funny, old man?" Matthew asked.

"Yeah, you two little clowns… that's what's funny." Pa said softly. His eyes cut over to us, "What did you want me to do?

Bear hug it?" He rolled his eyes and stood up slowly, "One bite! One scratch and you're done! We've seen this on the news. Now isn't the time to play hero…" Pa stared at us and then his lips turned upward into a shitty crooked smile as he said, "but you two know that, because I ain't see you boys running upstairs with your capes." My eyes went over to Matthew and then we both looked back at the basement door. In our panicked and fearful state we forgot the most helpless member of our family was lying upstairs, blissfully clueless to the horrors that were going on below her.

"Ma," I said softly and then took off toward the steps. This time it was Matthew's arms that wrapped around me, trying to keep me back.

"Adam! Don't be fucking crazy!" He shouted.

"Ma!" I screamed.

"Adam! Calm the fuc-" Matthew's words and everyone's hearts for that matter, were stopped cold by one loud chilling sound. A sound we never expected to hear at that moment.

THE SOUND OF A GUNSHOT.

"MA!" I screamed. The gunshot was followed by some light drilling sounds. I stood there staring up at the door as Matthew cautiously started making his way up the steps.

"Matthew! Get your ass down here!" Pa hissed. But Matt continued up the steps, one cautious footstep at a time. "Matthew!" Pa shouted.

"Listen to your daddy, Matty Boy!" A cold southern twang came from beyond the door. Then the laughter started. Two sets of it, a man and a woman.

"Yeah, I wouldn't get too close. I would hate for a bullet to mess up that pretty face of yours." The woman said.

"William? Ruby?" Matthew said softly. Matt's fingers pulled back on the latch, but when he pushed the door it didn't move. "William the door's stuck buddy." Matthew said with a laugh. "You mind-"

"Boy! I ain't your Goddamn buddy! I ain't your pal! I ain't your fucking friend!" William hollered. The female voice which I knew from anywhere laughed,

"All the doors and windows are bolted from the outside. We did a little DIY while y'all were sleeping." Ruby said. Matthew's fist started beating on the door,

"Open the fucking door! You Bitch!" Matthew shouted.

"Oh Matthew! That's a dirty, dirty mouth you got. Your Mama ain't teach you how to talk to a lady?" Ruby asked.

"Sis, that's a job for a daddy." William replied.

"I hope not, because then the whole lot of them are fucked." Ruby said and started to laugh.

"Mr. Rhodes!" William shouted. "Can you hear me well enough down there?" he asked. Our eyes darted toward Pa. He stood next to me at the bottom step.

I elbowed him and he rolled his eyes as he said, "Yeah."

"Good." William said softly. "You know I woke up this morning and I had no plans on ever seeing your shitshow of a family again. I said to myself 'Self! You are a man with many gifts. Many skills. You can do wonders.' I wanted to believe y'all firing me was a sign from God to move on and build elsewhere." William said.

"So, why didn't you?!" Matthew shouted.

"Because when I went to check on my little sister. To let her know, none of this was her fault. That we were given an opportunity to escape your family's prison of a life. I found her looping a bed sheet around her neck." William replied. There's very little in this world that shuts Matthew up, but that statement sure enough did. I don't know exactly what it did to me. My heart wasn't racing but it wasn't still. The only way I can describe it, is how a deer must feel. You know after a hunter shoots it and it's watching those camo pants coming closer, but it can't move. Then it sees that buck knife and all it wants to do is turn tail and run. All it wants is to be free of that moment. However a deer's heart feels in that moment, mine felt like that on cocaine.

"Ruby? I...I had no-" My words were cut short by the sound of a gunshot. Matthew bolted down the steps toward Pa and I.

"Don't you ever fucking talk to her again!" William shouted and the boy in me wanted to run and hide. If I'm honest, the man in me had the same idea. "Not you! Not your shithead brothers and for damn sure not that fucking old man down there!" We all stood there in silence. Because no matter what any of us wanted to do, at that moment we knew William was running the show now. "I begged her to come down off that chair. Hell, I threatened her! Told her I could knock her ass into the E.R before she could even think of stepping off that chair!" William shouted. Then we heard his voice soften as he said, "It was all talk. I was scared out of my mind. I didn't want that moment to be our last moment. I didn't wanna..." All men cry. Bad men, good men, weak men, strong men. We all do it. So I wasn't gonna judge William when he did it. Yet, while Matthew and I are brothers, we are not the same. The laughter started light at first like a kid in the back of the class and then it grew, "You laughing at me?" William asked.

I pushed Matthew and he pushed me back, "No. No one's laughing at you, William," I replied. Only because I felt anyone else's voice would have brought William down those steps, guns a blazing.

"Nothing I said would make her come down. She was hell-bent on killing herself, until..." William stopped talking. As much as his words were scaring the hell out of me. His silence scared me even more.

"Until what?" Matthew asked and I was sure that the door

was gonna fly open and bullets were gonna tear us in two, but you don't always need a weapon to tear someone in half.

Ruby knew that and she taught me that, "Until he said, we can kill them all, Ruby." Ruby said ever so sweetly.

"And that's what we aim to do." William said.

"You two are fucking crazy!" Pa shouted.

"No! Crazy is thinking you could fuck someone's world up and then toss them aside like a used condom," William said. I looked over at Pa and he couldn't even look at me. His eyes were locked on the bottom step. Like it was gonna come alive and save him from all this. "This isn't crazy, it's a blood bond. You understand what someone will do to protect their family, right Mr. Rhodes? Some people lie. Some people steal. Me, I'm part of a rare breed… that will kill and die for my blood." William said and then we heard the door unlatch. It slowly came open to show William and Ruby standing at the top of the steps in full tactical gear. Bulletproof vest, magazine pouches, knee pads; they came dressed for war. William's M4 pointed down at Pa and a red dot appeared on his chest. "The question is what breed are you, Mr. Rhodes?" William asked. Ruby's M4 came up and her red dot landed right in the middle of Matthew's head, "Because maybe if you were willing to die first, I might let your boys go." William said.

"If he dies, you'll let us go?" Matthew asked.

"He said maybe," Ruby replied. William laughed and then the two of them took slow steps back before closing the door.

"Someone has to pay for the sins of this family! I want an answer by the morning," William said.

"Tic Toc!" Ruby shouted. With that we heard footsteps, laughter and then nothing.

"You son of a bitch! I'll fucking kill you for this! You hear me! I'll fucking kill you!" Matthew shouted.

"Calm down Matt." Pa said softly and then Matthew's canon of rage had a whole new target. I was once again the only thing between Pa and a humbling moment of picking his teeth up off the floor.

"Calm down! Calm down! None of this would have happened if you fucking listened to me, in the first place!" Matthew shouted. He tossed me to the side and I slammed my elbow onto the claw end of an old hammer. They were arguing back and forth, but their words didn't seem to resonate with me. They were just empty shells as my mind focused on one thought.

One that echoed throughout my soul until my lips softly released it, "What did you do?" I asked. My words were ignored by the pissing contest that they were knee deep in. I was always ignored. Always thought of as this second class citizen who didn't need to know anything more than what he was told. Always taught to never have a voice, so I decided to raise it for once in my life, "What did you do!" I shouted and before they could react I sent that hammer sailing through the air. The blood came quickly. Then came the screaming. I watched as he crumbled down to the floor holding his face. I took a step forward and felt Matthew's hand go on my chest. The cursing never stopped. It went well into the night, but we never checked on him. I sat there staring at the blood rushing from his face as Pa attempted every so often to rip the claw hammer free of his cheek..

"SHE CAME into my office a month ago." Matthew whispered. It had been close to five or so hours since anyone said anything. Pa had stopped crying and was passed out on the floor next to Daniel, his shirt pressed against his cheek to stop the bleeding. I wanted to check on Danny, but I couldn't get over my rage enough to even make a motion toward Pa. I looked at Matthew and he let out a sigh as he continued, "Ruby said that the old man got a little fresh one night after drinking." Matthew laughed and shook his head, "She was telling me, my father was a monster and all I was thinking about was what kind of damage control was this gonna take?"

"Did he… Did he," I couldn't even bring myself to say the words.

"You know there's no reasoning with him when he's drunk. I'm sure she did her best to fight him off; knowing Ruby I know she fought the whole time." Matthew said and tousled his hair with his fingers before softly saying, "I thought looking out for the family was the right thing to do. So, I offered her some cash, but she declined and said she was gonna tell everyone. So, we fired her and William before she could."

"So that's the sin? That's what all the whispering has been about?" I asked and Matthew nodded before resting his head on the wall, "And your damage control was hoping they would just forget about it?" I asked.

"No, I fired them to make them look disgruntled if they ever did say anything. Send them off with a big bonus or something, It was better than Dad's plan." he said. I didn't ask what that plan was, because I already knew. However, as I sat on that cold basement floor facing another long hour in our billion dollar prison, I thought maybe Pa's plan wasn't that bad. I know God is always watching, but I hoped he wasn't in that moment, because I truly believed anything would have been better than letting William live.

"I'm hungry." I said softly.

"I'm starving." The faint words came from the bloody corner of the basement where Pa and Daniel lied.

"Danny?" Matthew said and we both rushed to his side. The mountain man didn't move, his body was still as he stared up at the light of the basement. My face came into his view and he closed his eyes.

"I'm gonna kill you shit-brick." Daniel said softly.

"You're gonna have to sit up first," I said.

We all laughed and then Daniel's eyes went over toward Pa, he looked back over at Matthew as he said, "What's up with the old man?"

"He got his face smashed in by a hammer." Matthew whispered.

"No shit! By who?" Daniel asked and I raised my hand slowly, "Is no one safe from your terror?" He asked and I sighed, shaking my head.

"I think we should do it," Matthew said.

"Do what?" I asked. Matthew's eyes came upon me and no words needed to be spoken. I shook my head and got to my feet, "No, we're not doing that," I said.

Matthew shot to his feet and shouted, "What other choice do we have? You heard William, he might let us go!" I rolled my eyes and looked over at Pa. Matthew started walking toward him and I stood in his way once again, "It's him or us," Matthew said softly. I heard Pa shuffling behind me and then Daniel slowly sat up for the first time in hours.

I took a step back and shook my head as I softly said, "We're a family."

Before I got the chance to see the reaction on Matthew's face, the basement door opened and he took off, speeding up the steps. I ran after him, but came to a stop when I saw the barrel of William's M4 rifle being pointed down at us. The red dot found a nice home on Matthew's chest.

"Back the fuck up, Matty Boy!" William shouted. The door opened up wider and Ruby came into view with a large pot in her hands, "Unless you're coming up to be the first to die?" He asked.

"I wish," Ruby said. She looked down at me and smiled, "Adam, I made you boys some stew."

"I'll take it," Matthew said softly as he put out his hands.

Ruby stared at his palms for a moment before looking back up into his eyes, "It's Adam or none of you little shits eat!" She screamed. I've loved Ruby pretty much all my life. I knew her favorite color, her zodiac sign, even her shoe size. But I missed the moment when my beautiful angel fell from grace. I wondered how long she was crying out for help with no one answering her? I wondered how many studio sessions she wished she could avoid? How many fake smiles did she have to put on? I slowly started making my way up the steps past Matthew. I came up to the top and Ruby placed the pot in my hands. Then she put a set of spoons on the lid. "I did the best I could with what I had," she said. I stared down at the lid for an awkward moment trying to think of something to say.

"I'm sorry for what they did," I said softly. Ruby's hand rested on mine and she leaned in. As her body came closer I saw the barrel of William's M4 slowly turn toward me.

With one jerk of a finger he could end my life and part of me wished he would, but instead of a bullet in my chest, I got a soft whisper in my ear, "All we want is him." Ruby leaned back and her soft pink lips brushed along my cheek and sent a chill through me. I was in such a trance that I didn't even notice when they closed the door and locked it. I was standing there staring at the lid of the pot.

"Umm dipshit! You mind bringing the food down?" Daniel shouted. I turned slowly on my heels and then started down the steps thinking about Ruby's soft words. Her and Matthew seemed to be on the same dark path. Everyone started digging into the sweet brown stew, but I wrestled with thoughts in my head. The world was changing, it was getting colder, but that didn't mean we had to get colder with it. We could stand our ground and figure something out, or we could stubble in the dark with the rest of the world. I watched as my father took a bite of a large chunk of meat, his eyes didn't dare meet any of ours. We were family, we could make it through this. That's what I wanted to tell myself but even if we could, Ma couldn't. Ruby and William had no idea when she needed her shots, or when it was time to change her bags. The longer we stayed down here the more likely she was going to die up there. With that one thought I stepped into the darkness.

"Ruby says all they want is Pa." I said softly. The spoons stopped their frantic shoveling of stew and everyone's eyes fell onto me. Everyone but Pa who kept his gaze on the floor. "We give them Pa and they'll let us go," I said. There were no words, just empty stares at one another. I don't know how you could form words for that kind of moment. Pa slowly started to get to his feet and Matthew did the same.

"So, that's how it's gonna be?" Pa asked softly. He looked at Matt and Pa took a step back and shook his head. "No! No! That's not happening! Not after all I've done for you! For all of you!" He shouted.

Matthew looked at me and I shifted my jaw for a moment before I looked at Pa's bloody face and softly said, "It's your sin, you should answer for it."

With that Matthew and I rushed forward toward Pa. He backed up as far as he could till his back was against the wall and like any cornered animal he fought. I took his first hit, right to my jaw and went down fast. Matthew took one to the arm but he fired back with a blow to Pa's gut. I watched as Matthew unloaded fist after fist on the old man. Years of resentment and anger finally finding a way free from his body. There's no telling how many things he had to cover up, how many lies he had to tell to keep Pa above water. For years the old man was drowning in his sins and he was pulling Matthew down right along with him. I got to my feet and joined in. Daniel didn't say a word as my white sneakers started to turn red from the blood.

I sent each kick flying into his already pummeled face. Bones cracked. Screams were heard. Tears were shed from all sides. I turned and picked up the hammer off the floor but then Matthew's hand came out toward me.

"That's enough." Matthew said. I dropped the hammer and listened to the metal echo through the basement as the head hit the floor. We got down low and lifted our bloody mess of a father off of the ground. One shaky step after another we made our way up to the basement door, "Just sit him up," Matthew said softly and we did.

I stared at the red balloon that was once his right eye socket and I bit my lip as I said, "I'm sorry Pa." I heard a gurgle come from his mouth as a stream of blood pushed from his lips. I stood up and pounded on the door. Then Pa's hand shot up grabbing a hold of my neck. My eyes came down to see a small bit of hazel staring back at me. His fingers tightened around my neck. I could feel his nails breaking into my skin. My Adam's apple had no room to move. I was choking. The last bit of energy he had in him, he was using it to kill me. I felt a sudden rush of pain in the back of my eyeballs as my head started to fall back. Just when I thought I was a goner the basement door opened up and William slammed the butt of his rifle into Pa's head. His hand fell and I went tumbling back into Matthew's open arms. We watched as they dragged Pa into the house and slammed the door, locking it once again.

"You alright?" Matthew asked. My hand rubbed along my neck and I nodded. But I wasn't alright, who could be. I had just turned over my father to a pair of psychos in hopes of saving my own life. I beat my father, till he couldn't stand and his last memory of me might be of him wanting to kill me.

I turned around and started down the steps as I softly said, "I'm alright."

We all sat around the stew and started eating once again.

IT HAD BEEN a few hours since we last saw Pa or anyone from the other side of that door. While a few hours isn't much time in the normal world, we were far past normal at that point. We gave up Pa in hopes that William's 'maybe' was closer to a yes than a no.

"They're not gonna let us out," Matthew said softly.

"No, they have no reason to keep us down here." I replied.

"They got twenty to twenty-five years of reasons, shit-brick. They don't want to go to jail over this," Daniel said.

"There aren't any more jails," I said.

"Why? Because we saw one fucking zombie? For all we know they took care of the outbreak and the world is moving on just like it always does," Daniel said.

"So why keep us down here? Why keep us alive at all?" I asked. Matthew shrugged and rested his head on the wall. We all sat in silence for a moment before I softly said, "I wonder how Ma is doing."

Matthew's eyes came over to me and he placed his hand on my shoulder, "I'm sure she's fine." Matthew said softly. He coughed and then I coughed. My throat felt tight and itchy. I looked over at Daniel who had started coughing as well. It was then I noticed how grey the air looked. I walked closer to the steps and I could smell the smoke. I made my way up the wooden steps.

I was face to face with the door. I took a moment and then I started pounding on it, "William! Ruby!" I shouted. My hand continued to pound on the door. "William! Open up!" I shouted. I could hear Matthew and Daniel quickly coming up behind me. We all started coughing as the smoke seemed to be pushing faster into the room. "William!" I shouted. Matthew pulled me aside as he started slamming his hands into the door.

"Ruby! Open this fucking door!" Matthew shouted. Yet, there was no answer, no sound whatsoever. All that could be heard were our heartbeats and the door as it shook under Matthew's fist. "Open the fucking door!"

"Move," Daniel said. With those words Matthew and I took a step back and allowed the mountain that was our older brother to make his way toward the door. His hand took hold of the door knob and he shook it for a moment. "It's warm," he said. Then he took a step back and lowered his shoulder. I watched as his shoulder went slamming into the thick wooden door. One violent ram after another was sent by Daniel. We all knew what this moment meant. If they weren't responding to this then they were gone. We heard the wood start to split and then Matthew joined in on the attack. One giant ram later and the door went flying open. Daniel and Matthew hit the floor just as fast as the black smoke hit our nostrils. It was filling the house, but it was clear that the fire was upstairs. I stepped over them and started toward the staircase.

"Where the hell are you going!" Daniel shouted.

"I'm gonna go get Ma!" I shouted.

"Don't be dumb!" He shouted. I heard both my brothers calling my name, but I continued on. I closed my eyes slightly because the heat and the smoke were causing them to burn. I felt my way to Mama's room and when my hand hit the doorknob, I quickly pulled it back. The metal was burning hot.

"Ma!" I shouted. I started to kick the door. I didn't know what to expect. I wasn't even sure what I was doing. I just knew she needed me. I kicked the door one more time and it pushed open, then my heart stopped. The bed was engulfed in flames and the room was quickly following behind it.

"Adam!" Matthew shouted. He grabbed a hold of me as I fought to run into the room.

"Ma!" I screamed. Sweat poured down my face as the flames made their way toward the door. Matthew kept dragging me back, pulling me down the hall. It was a back and forth fight until Daniel came and tossed me over his shoulder. I kept screaming, "Ma!" all the way down the steps. We made it to the front door but it wouldn't move. It was bolted shut from the other side like Ruby said.

"What the fuck are we gonna do?" Matthew asked.

Daniel tossed me down on the floor and he bashed his elbow through the window, knocking out the glass. He started pushing the shards of glass onto the floor. He turned around to look at us. Blood was running down his arm as he shouted, "Move your asses."

We all went through the window one by one. I was last and as I coughed and stared at the staircase I honestly thought of just staying there and letting the flames take me too. My eyes went toward the kitchen and I could see a pool of blood with two bodies lying among the red. One was Zombie Travis, all burned and freakish looking. The other body was Pa, I could tell from the gold watch that was still on his wrist. They might have done the deed but it was his sons that truly killed him. I turned and hopped through the window. When I came through on the other side I saw Matthew and Daniel standing there staring out at the driveway. I took a step closer and I could see them. Ruby and William, sitting on the hood of Pa's mustang, with a front row seat to watch our home burn.

"Damn. Y'all got out faster than I thought." William said before pointing his weapon at us, "Maybe you were right, Sis, we should have started the fire on the first floor."

"Told you," Ruby replied.

I pushed past my brothers and I pointed at her, "How could you do that? To her! Ma had nothing to do with this! How could you Ruby?" I shouted. Ruby stared at me and rolled her eyes before sliding off the hood of the car clapping her hands slowly.

"You're cute. It's sweet how you think the world works." She said, Matthew took a step forward and Ruby sighed, "Thinking you could just walk around here, like a gift. Without letting me take a peek inside?"

"What the hell are you going on about?" Daniel shouted.

"You three been down there for damn near a day, he didn't tell you the juicy details about what he did? All the shit he said before he raped me!" Ruby shouted.

"I'm sorry for what Pa did to you, but we… but Ma! She didn't have anything to do with that!" I shouted.

"Pa?" William said.

"Your Daddy was a snake, who thought he could pay me to keep my mouth shut," Ruby said. William started walking towards us with his M4 aimed. "He thought because y'all had money that it was gonna solve everything. Like it could give back what you took from me!" Ruby screamed. Then I heard it. It wasn't a whisper, more like a dirty cat call you heard in the middle of the night from some drunk frat boys.

"You know you liked it." Matthew said and I took a step back.

"What?" I said softly and Matthew looked at me. There was a small smile on his face and then he looked back at Ruby.

"You loved it, Ruby. I don't know what all this is really about, but it ain't about that." Matthew said and then we watched as the red dot moved to the middle of Matthew's chest.

"You raped me!" Ruby screamed.

"And now you're gonna pay!" William shouted. A loud blast was heard but it wasn't the one I expected. Mama's window exploded, sending glass flying. It was only a small moment that delayed William's reaction by a second but it was all Daniel needed as he rushed William, picking him up into the air and slamming him down onto the ground. The two of them rolled back and forth on the lawn.

"Get off him!" Ruby shouted. I looked over at Pa's car to see the handle of an M4 sticking up from the passenger seat. Ruby's hazel eyes fell on me, then they darted over to the car. Next thing I knew we were both racing toward it. I was just a second faster as I pulled out the rifle and pointed it at her.

"Back the hell up!" I shouted. Ruby's hands went up and she slowly started taking steps backwards. I turned the muzzle of the gun towards William and Daniel, "Alright! That's enough!" I shouted but they kept rolling, so I fired a warning shot into the air and the pair came to a quick stop. Matthew walked over to them picking up William's M4. "Get over there by your brother." I said softly.

"You alright?" Matthew asked.

"Yeah," Daniel said. They both walked over toward me. I kept my red dot on Ruby and Matthew kept his on William.

"You don't have to do this. I told you all we want is him." Ruby said.

I looked over at Matthew and then looked back at Ruby, "Well you can't have him." I said. I felt Matthew's eyes on me, was he proud? Was he happy that his little brother was standing up for him? I don't know, I don't think I'll ever know what goes on inside his head. "You killed my father and my mother." I said softly, "And now you gotta pay for your sins." I said.

"Any last words?" Matthew asked.

William's hands were up along with Ruby's. He smiled and nodded, "Yeah, just one. How did that stew taste?" William asked, Ruby's head turned to look at him. "Was it sweet? Maybe something Mama would make?" William said as he started laughing.

"What the fuck are you laughing at!" Daniel yelled.

"You ate your Mama!" William shouted. "You ate your Mama!" His words still wake me up in the middle of the night, that crazed scream. I can't get it out of my head. Matthew pulled the trigger and sent a bullet flying into William's head. Ruby jumped and looked over at me.

"Please, Adam!" She cried and I pulled the trigger. I watched her body fly back and tumbled over onto the ground. I should have turned my rifle on him or myself. If I was a real man I would have done that a long time ago, but I'm more like my dad than I like to admit. I'm a coward, who just wants to do right by his family. Daniel said I ain't been right since then, he said I'm broken, and maybe I am. We loaded up in the car and drove off. I didn't tell anyone this, because I guess I felt I owed her something but I saw Ruby get up. I don't know what happened to her, but I hope she's doing better than we are, I hope she got away from the sin. Daniel said he had some buddies down by Ft. Gordon that could help us out, but the car crapped out on us before then. We ended up coming across this nice traveling circus. They took us in. Might be why we still keep them around.

I think about putting a bullet in them, but then I see all those people who saw three lost men and took pity on them. They didn't have to do that, so I just can't kill them. Daniel doesn't do it because Matthew tells him not to. Matt says they come in handy. He says they're good at scaring people. Girls, they're good at scaring girls and Matt, well he likes the fear.

I'm sorry, I'm going on and on. I'm sure you three just wanna know why you're hanging upside down over these buckets. I wish I could tell you it's a joke. That this is all to scare you and you'll be okay. Y'all must feel like a deer right now, wanting to turn tail and run. But you can't, because I won't let you. I'm the only thing stopping you, so in a way, I'm like the hunter's bullet. Y'all are gonna die here. It's gonna be painful and bloody. They're gonna do some really bad things to y'all. So, I just thought instead of hanging here and wondering what's gonna happen next. I'd keep you entertained with some stories.

What was that? No, I'm sorry I can't remove your gag. Matthew would be really mad at me. He runs the show now, he's The Ringmaster.

QUICK BITE: THE HANGED MAN (FLASH FICTION MADE FOR REANIMATED RUMBLE)

Two shots rang out through the dark, shattering the silence that had settled over Corpse Wood. The town, still recovering from the drunken revelries of the night, sprung back to life with a vengeance. The haunting sound pierced the air, stirring a sense of urgency in the deputy, who stepped out into the cool night.

"What the hell is going on?"

It was a rare blessing to enjoy such a pleasant evening in Corpse Wood. The stifling heat had retreated to some other pit of hell, granting the town a temporary reprieve. The deputy had hoped for a quiet shift, devoid of the usual drunken brawls that required his intervention. However, as he surveyed the town shrouded in darkness, the whispers and shouts of its awakening inhabitants shattered any hope of sleep.

A woman rushed onto the candle lit porch of the sheriff's station, clutching her petticoat tightly to conceal her nightwear. Panting, she urgently grasped the deputy's hands, concern etched on her face. "There's been a shooting at Molly's!" she exclaimed.

"Who was shot?" The deputy hollered.

"Big Ben" The woman replied.

Out of all the things the deputy thought he would hear that night, 'Ben's been shot' was not one of them. Ben was what one might call... an evil man. Now, one would never say that to Ben's face, but in the shadowy corners of a crowded saloon, through whispered lips, one might paint him with words like wicked or sinister. So, the deputy couldn't believe that anyone in Corpse Wood could muster up the courage to yell at Ben, much less shoot him twice. But there he was, faced down on Molly's bedroom floor with two bullets buried in his flesh. One in his back, which the deputy reckon went through his heart and helped with the killing, and one in his head which the deputy knew helped with the killing.

"God damn," the deputy whispered softly, stunned by the sight.

"It was that colored man," a voice emerged from the dimly lit room. Molly, seated in a dark corner near the window, revealed herself.

The deputy gaze went from Ben's lifeless body; who had one shoe on and whose bullet holed head was sticking out through the doorway, to Molly as he tried to process the revelation. He had to step over Ben's body to enter the room. "Colored man?" he repeated, seeking clarification.

Molly nodded, taking a drag from her cigarette. The smoldering ember taunted the deputy with its fiery glow, akin to the eye of the devil. "Ben's boys went after him," she disclosed.

As if Molly's words were a dinner bell ringing in the distance, the deputy heard the commotion caused by Ben's boys in the town square. They clamored for a rope, signaling their intentions loud and clear. The deputy descended the steps and hurried through the closed saloon, the cool night air refreshing against his face. There, he witnessed the frightened colored man, surrounded by Ben's vengeful posse.

"What do y'all think you're doing? Leave that fella be!" The deputy shouted.

"The boy shot Ben dead, and he's gonna hang," one of Ben's boys called out defiantly.

The rope had arrived, fashioned into a noose, and placed around the young man's neck. The deputy took a step forward, only to hear the chilling sound of hammers being cocked on sidearms.

"Maybe so, but that man deserves a trial, and Ben deserves justice. We don't condemn innocent men to death in Corpse Wood, you know that," the deputy proclaimed, his voice steady.

"Ben's getting his justice... Molly witnessed it all. So you can step aside and watch him hang, or you can step up and join him, and I'll bury you right next to the colored bastard if it makes you feel better," the hangman declared.

"I didn't do it, sir. I swear," the man whimpered, his lips swollen and bloodied.

"Well, deputy?" The hangman asked.

The deputy spat at the ground, his resolve hardening, and without a word, he turned and retreated into the saloon. Settling onto a barstool, he poured himself a shot of whiskey when he heard the man scream. Then he poured himself another shot, when the screaming stopped. The deputy waited in the saloon's darkness refusing to acknowledge the horrors unfolding outside. Unwilling to even look up from his glass into the mirror, fearful of the man that would be looking back at him. Instead, he raised the glass to his lips, taking a slow sip, savoring the warmth of the burn as it traveled down his throat, as a scream filled the saloon.

"Ben's..." the woman began but was quickly interrupted by the deputy.

"Ben's up?" The deputy interjected.

The petticoat-clad woman nodded, attempting to grab the

deputy's arm, but he pulled away and poured himself another shot.

"Well, he's just the first of many, I reckon," The deputy hissed.

"He's trying to kill Molly!" The woman shouted.

"Most likely because Molly killed him as he was leaving. Probably owed her money. Now we have an innocent man lying in our street, and you know what that means?" The deputy looked over at the confused woman and sighed, pouring himself another drink. "It means we'll be dealing with the dead until sunrise... which means I need to wake the sheriff."

The deputy rose slowly, taking a step toward the door. However, he couldn't resist the temptation and grabbed the whiskey bottle, ensuring it accompanied him on his hellish journey. Pushing through the saloon doors, he confronted the icy chill of the night. Ben's men stood over the hanged man's lifeless body, they went about trying to pull him free of the dirt's hold, but the deputy knew it was a futile endeavor; the ground held the man until sunrise.

"Deputy... we-" one of Ben's men began.

"Leave the body be and go help Molly before Ben turns her into one of them," The deputy said without looking at Ben's men. Then the night air filled with a chorus of mournful moans, carried on the wind, "On second thought, head to the cemetery and hold them off while I fetch the sheriff... and boys!" he called out.

"Yeah, deputy?" They said in unison.

"Try your damnedest not to die," he said with conviction, stepping into the darkness, leaving behind a trail of fading whispers and the taste of whiskey on his lips.

UNFIT (FIRST PUBLISHED IN MAD LIKE ME)

*S*top fidgeting and sit up straight. You want him to help you right?

"Calm down, Sarah" Dr. Alexander's soothing voice broke through my internal turmoil. His warm, dark hand rested on my golden brown fist, and his finger gently rubbed along my skin, as if trying to extract the anger within me. Despite his kindness, there was no calming the storm inside of me.

"Due to Mr. Connors' interaction or lack thereof, we, the court, find him mentally unfit to stand trial," declared the judge. His gavel came down with a thunderous smack, and just like that, it was over.

"Murderer!" one woman screamed, her voice echoing through the courtroom, soon joined by another.

The judge's ruling unleashed a wave of emotions within the courtroom. Mr. Connors, or Mr. Donald William Connors, as his sweet landlord had called him, was more or less free. He would spend the rest of his years in a mental institution, but that was nothing compared to the lethal injection. I knew this because I was a nurse at Saint Andrew's Hospital for the Mentally Ill, where Dr. Alexander serves as my boss. We had come to ensure that justice was served to Mr. Connors, whom the papers had dubbed 'The Sweet Water Devil.'

"It's turning into a madhouse, let's go," Dr. Alexander suggested. I glanced around the room, observing the clenched fists, much like my own, shooting into the air one after another, their fists moving in hypnotic rhythm to their chanting.

"Murderer!"

"Murderer!"

I wanted to urge them to remain calm. Drown out the fires that were roaring within them, to save their voices, because the Devil will get his due. But I can't, so I don't.

"Let's go," I replied, and we swiftly exited the courtroom.

I heard the police arrested three people. Isn't that a slap in the face of justice? Your loved one's killer gets to walk out, while you're placed in handcuffs.

DURING THE CAR RIDE, a heavy silence enveloped us. We skirted around the elephant tap-dancing in the room, or perhaps I was the one evading it. Maybe a part of me desired to carry that burden, to have it dance in my life indefinitely. However, when the car came to a halt, I realized my desires no longer mattered. Dr. Alexander quickly shot the elephant dead with his statement.

"Well, this is it. He's gonna be in our care for the foreseeable future," Dr. Alexander stated. He shifted in his seat, turning to face me. My gaze remained fixed on the falling leaves that gracefully descended onto the car's hood. His rich, ebony skin contrasted with my light brown complexion, as his hands gently enveloped mine, and his eyes locked onto mine.

Kiss him.

"If you have any reservations about the plan, then now would be the time to voice them, because there is no turning back once this starts," he said.

Just nod. No, answer him. Nodding seems so passive.

"This needs to happen, Dr. Alexander," I replied, running my finger along the back of his hand. Our brown eyes remained locked onto each other until he broke into a smile, shifting his gaze to our entwined hands.

"You can call me Calvin. After everything that's happened, I think you can call me by my first name," he said.

He wants you to say his name. Go on, say it.

"Thank you," I said, withdrawing my hands as I stepped out of the car. The door closed behind me, leaving me standing in the cool autumn air as Dr. Alexander drove off down the road. That night, for the first time since that monster known as 'The Sweet Water Devil' took my Dallas, I slept.

"Patient Donald William Connors?" I read off the name slowly, suppressing my body's primal urge to choke on it. His sleazy lawyer stood up and walked over to me. I held my clipboard tightly, never letting my eyes off the monster known as Mr. Connors. He sat there, his pale skin marred by red spots and scars, his buggy blue eyes fixed on the floor between his feet.

"I'm sure you are aware from his file, Mr. Connors doesn't speak." the lawyer said.

I nodded, "Oh yes, I recall Dr. Alexander telling me that," I replied.

"You've spoken with Dr. Alexander?" He asked.

"Yes," I matter-of-factly responded.

"Is he here? I would like to speak with him," He inquired.

"No," I said.

"No, he's not here, or no, I can't speak with him?" He pressed.

I smiled and lowered my clipboard to my side as I looked back at the monster. His hair was dirty and shaggy, and a gray and white beard aged him beyond his years. Seeing him sitting there staring into space made him appear harmless, yet I knew better.

"Hello," the lawyer said as he snapped his fingers in my face.

Oh, let this mother fucker have it!

"The doctor! Isn't here!" I shouted. The monster's head slowly picked up. His eyes scanned over my body as I'm sure they had countless other bodies. I leaned into the lawyer and softly said, "I know what you and the doctor have agreed upon. No worries, your client is in good hands," I said. When I leaned back, I saw it. It was faint, almost so much so that I believed I had imagined it, but I swore the monster smiled at me.

The male orderlies cautiously approached the monster and handcuffed him, pulling him from his seat.

"Are those necessary?" The lawyer asked.

I smiled and turned on my heels, following behind the orderlies. As the guard buzzed us through the large doors, we were greeted by a crowd of curious onlookers. Some in robes, some in single-color jumpsuits, and one in his birthday suit.

"Good God! Can someone get Timothy some clothes!" I shouted into the echoing halls. A nurse started rushing over toward the naked man who waved his hand and, umm, his little member at me.

"Hi, Ms. Sarah," he said.

"Hi, Timothy," I hissed.

The patients had limited access to the outside world. They walked the grounds, and some had visitors, but for the most part, the only time they got to see the world beyond these walls was during television time. From ten in the morning until four in the afternoon, they got lost in the images of the real world. We mostly left the TV on daytime shows or cartoons, but once the murders started, it seemed every channel was talking about 'The Sweet Water Devil.' We did our best to avoid the case altogether, but every day someone new would be watching it. Slowly the monster became a star and a devil in their eyes, and now their star has fallen and walks the same halls as them.

"What room is he in, Nurse Sarah?" The large orderlies asked.

My eyes went down to the clipboard, and I shuffled through a few papers before saying, "The ninth ward, room C." When my clipboard came down, the two men were staring at me, wearing a mixed look of wonder and disbelief. "Is there a problem?" I asked.

"No, but there isn't anyone in the ninth ward at the moment," the orderly replied.

I laughed and crossed my arms, pressing the board to my chest, "He'll hardly be isolated. We'll just have to take a longer walk to get him for social activities. Due to his high profile, Dr. Alexander feels it would be best to keep him away from the others until the shock and awe wear off," I said.

A longer walk, more like a hike down into hell. No one is going to hear him down there... No one.

When the elevator doors opened, Dr. Alexander was there waiting. The door to room C was wide open. I watched as the orderlies walked the monster into the room. I stood in the hall as Dr. Alexander spoke with him. It was the normal in-processing jargon.

Nothing is normal about this.

The door closed and the orderlies started toward the elevator. I took my first steps toward the monster's cage. My hand came out and my fingertips brushed the cool metal of the door before Dr. Alexander's hand rested on my own.

"Not now," He said softly.

No, no! Now is fine! Now is perfect!

"You're right," I said softly.

Dumb bitch!

I returned to the main floor and continued about my day. It was a hard task to do; my mind kept escaping its tasks and drowning in all the wicked things the monster did to her. Her name was Dallas, and she was the prettiest star to ever fall from the sky. She came into my life during a very dark point, a darkness that she didn't need to be a part of. She was better off without me. I would see her and her parents from time to time at the park or the mall. They didn't see me, I didn't want them to. She was happy, and I wanted her to stay that way. But then the monster rolled into our lives, and nothing was the same. I had to pretend all was well for weeks, while I was dying inside, and now I have only a few more days of repeating that fake form of life.

TODAY IS THE DAY!

"You pulling a double, Sarah?" Nurse Jackie asked. Her question pulled me out of the fog that kidnapped my day.

I nodded and rolled my shoulders as I said, "Our V.I.P guest needs a personal nightly nurse. Doctor's orders."

"You're a better woman than me. No way would I go down there with that fucking sicko," Nurse Jackie said. She pulled a pack of cigarettes out of her pocket and quickly started slapping the pack into her open hand repeatedly. "I mean he lit one poor girl on fire. I'm just happy I don't have any kids to worry about," she said and then the slapping stopped as she stared at me. "Fuck, Sarah, I'm sorry. I mean-"

"It's fine," I said and shoved my hands into my pockets.

We both awkwardly nodded for a moment before she asked, "Adaptions are good, I've thought about it… What you did was good for…? What's her name again?"

Dallas you stupid, heartless, little…

"Dallas. It's Dallas." I said as I walked off towards the elevator.

"Goodnight!" She shouted.

You should flip her off.

I make my way to the ninth ward, and as the elevator opens, Dr. Alexander is there waiting.

"Now?" I say softly.

"Soon, we have to wait for the night staff to clear out. Then it's just us and the graveyard shift," he said softly.

My eyes glanced at the large metal C that sat over the monster's cage. I shoved my hands in my pockets and felt the cool glass bottles tumble between my fingers. "Have you spoken to him?" I asked.

"Somewhat, he's keeping up the act of mutism like his lawyer advised him to," Dr. Alexander said.

"Does he know you coached his lawyer?" I asked.

"I believe so. Nonetheless, him remembering me isn't why we're here," he said as his hazel eyes fell upon me. "We're here to make sure he never forgets Dallas. To make sure he knows the pain he put you and her through," he said. His hand extended, softly running along my elbow, sending a chill through my bare skin. I couldn't look at him, my gaze fixed on the floor.

"He's a monster," I whispered.

"He is the worst kind," Dr. Alexander's eyes returned to the metal door, his jawline tightening under his salt-and-peppered beard. "The kind of monster that preys on the weak, that takes with no concern for anyone else." His eyes met mine again, and his lips attempted a half-hearted smile. "But this monster will only be a memory after tonight," he said.

His hand clasped mine. "You promise?" I asked softly.

"I promise," he replied, and our lips met for the first time. *Finally.*

AN HOUR PASSED, and as I buttoned up my shirt, I began to question why I was truly here. Could the monster mean so much to me that I was willing to throw away all I've worked for? All Calvin has worked for? Was this genuinely about justice, or was I using this as a means to get closer? Using her memory to get closer to him?

She's gone, and it's because of that monster! Now! Now is the time!

"I'm sorry you weren't in her life the way you wanted," Calvin said softly.

I glanced at him over my shoulder and smiled, "She was an amazing little girl. She had the most incredible green eyes," I softly said as my fingers fastened the last of my buttons.

"Amazing like her mother," Calvin whispered. He put his hand into his pocket, and I listened as his footsteps echoed through the ghostly wing of the hospital. The ninth ward hadn't been used for some time. Padded cells and other trademarks of the ninth ward were classified as inhuman, making it a most fitting location for our monstrous guest.

"Now?" I asked.

"Now," Calvin replied softly. His hand emerged from his white coat pocket with a set of large padded handcuffs. He stood in front of the door, and I stood off to the side, hiding much like the first time the monster and I had met. Calvin's hand slammed onto the metal door, and he shouted, "Hands!" We stared at the metal door under the dim glow of the fluorescent lights. With no answer or sign of life coming from beyond the door, not a shuffle, not a moan, I don't think I could even hear breathing in the moment.

Maybe he killed himself.

I jumped when the monster's hands pushed through the metal slot by Calvin's knees. His tattooed forearms faced up at us. I could see bold black letters pushing out from his skin.

Die Young? Well isn't that sweet and fitting.

The handcuffs came down around his wrist, and Calvin pulled at the straps, tightening them. Before the monster could recoil, Calvin's gentle hold turned into a vice grip. His fingernails pressed deep into the pink, soft meat of the monster's arm. My hand went into my pocket, and my fingers brushed along the glass bottles. I quickly pulled one out to unite with the syringe in my left hand.

"Do you know why you're here, Mr. Connors?" Calvin asked.

A tug was attempted, but Calvin stood strong.

"I'm here to be fixed," the monster replied.

Fixed? Evil can't be fixed, only removed!

"Your lawyer and I came to an agreement. I did my part and saved you from the needle," Calvin said, and I rammed the needle into the monster's forearm, pushing the clear liquid into his vile skin, right in the middle of the dark, bold D. The tattooed arms quickly pulled back through the slot, and Calvin smiled, "Now is when you uphold your end of the bargain," he said.

"Son of a bitch!" the monster hollered.

That's what I've been waiting for. Hurt him! Kill him!

Echoing throughout the dead hallway was a loud and chilling bang. The syringe rolled from my fingers and danced along the concrete floor. Another thunderous bang was heard, and this time the door shook. I backed away slowly.

No, no, don't run now. This is when the fun starts.

"Sarah, open the door to the med-bay," Calvin said, but I couldn't move. I want this or I wanted it. My eyes didn't lift from the little slot until Calvin's voice came once again, "Sarah!" Calvin shouted and my head spun. "The door, get the door," he said.

I ran down the hall because-

Because you want this to happen.

No! I mean yes, yes I do, but-

But nothing, this has to happen. There is no other way around it. If you stop now, he'll never love you. If you stop now, they'll put us in a cell right next to that monster. Do you want that?

No!

Good, then open the door.

I pulled the keys from my pocket, my fingers trembling as I tossed metal aside in hopes of finding the right one. I heard a click, and my neck snapped toward the sound. Calvin opened the monster's cage, and his limp body made a sickening thump when it hit the floor. Calvin stood over him, mouthing something, but I wasn't sure what it was. The key slipped into the hole, and the tumbler twisted and turned.

Open Sesame.

My fingers searched the cool white blocks that lined the med-bay through total and complete darkness until I ran over the comforting and memorable feeling of a light switch. I hit it, and the room flickered to life. It was an all-white room, with silver objects popping out from every corner. Pans, saws, and drills, but one object stood out above the rest.

It's an operating table... Calling Dr. Alexander.

Stop!

You stop!

Calvin came into the room, with the monster hung over his shoulders like a fireman carrying a survivor. But Calvin had far less care as he dropped the body down onto the floor. The monster's head slammed into the once-white tiles, and blood started to pour from the back of the monster's skull. Calvin scooped him back up once again and motioned his head toward the table.

"Get the straps ready." Calvin said.

And so I did. We strapped him down tightly to the table, and I rammed a towel deep into his mouth.

Have I told you how smart you are?

No, never. Not even once.

Well you are, you're a very, very smart girl.

Thank you.

You're welcome.

"HELLO, sunshine. We thought you would never join us. Sarah thought you were dead, but I had more faith in you," Calvin said. His gloved hands went onto the monster's face, holding its eyes open while shining a light in them. "Yeah, he's good to go!" Calvin shouted as he clapped his hands together.

That was the moment the monster noticed the blood on Calvin's hands, dripping from his gloved fingers. The monster's head slowly rolled over to me, our eyes locked. In his eyes, I could see a light icy blue slowly pulling out of a haze. In my eyes, he could see—

Fear?

No! Hate. In my eyes he could see hate.

"Hello," I said softly. He continued to stare at me, without acknowledging my greeting, so I shouted, "Hello!" His eyes closed, and he took a deep swallow and then mumbled something. I cupped my hand to my ear and said, "I'm sorry, what was that?" Calvin pointed at the towel in his mouth, and I slapped the side of my head. "Silly me," I said as I pulled the cloth from his mouth.

Idiot!

"Hello," The monster said.

"My name is Sarah, and I will be your nurse for this evening," I said with a smile, folding my hands together and nodding, "Tonight is a very big night."

"Is it?" The monster asked.

"Oh, yes, it is Mr. Connors," Calvin replied.

Tell him why.

"Tonight we're going to remove a very deadly cancer from the world. A nasty little one that's killed eighteen girls," I said with a gasp as I put my hand over my mouth. The monster's eyes didn't show any emotion. Then again, I wasn't sure what emotion I wanted to see. I didn't know what fear or terror actually looked like. His eyes were focused on me as my hand dropped from my lips. "This cancer is a real threat to anyone it comes in contact with. So we are doing the world an amazingly good service by removing it, Mr. Connors," I finished.

The monster glared at Calvin, and then the monster's body jolted from a still onlooker, to a frantic man as it pulled at the leather straps.

"Oh, my!" I said, my hand over my chest.

"You son of a bitch! You said I'd be out in a few months. You said if I just played ball I'd—" The monster's words were cut off by Calvin's laughter. Calvin's bloody hand came up and wiped some sweat away from his eyebrow, leaving a streak of red on his forehead.

Sexy.

"I know what I said, son. Sadly, you are as stupid as you look." Calvin's hand came up with a shining silver object under the operating lights. "You didn't really think I would send something like you back out onto the streets, did you?" Calvin asked, and the monster stared. "Did you!" Calvin shouted. The shining object came closer to the monster's face, giving both him and me a better view. It was a scalpel, a nice sharp scalpel that Calvin slowly started to bring closer to the monster's eye.

Take his fucking eye out!

"Take his eye out!" I shouted.

Calvin's eyes came over to me, and he smiled. There was no turning back now. The only way to come out of this alive was to continue down this wicked path we had created.

"First, I want to play a game," Calvin said. He leaned forward and rested his chin on his forearms, crossed over the monster's chest. "I want to see what kind of soul you have."

Monster's don't have souls.

"What do you mean?" I asked.

Calvin smiled while staring at the monster, "I want to know more about his victims." Calvin shook his head and stood upright, "No, that's not it. I want to see how much he knows about his victims."

The room fell silent, or maybe I went deaf; I honestly couldn't tell in that moment.

A game? What kind of sick fuck is he?

He's not sick; he's unique.

Yeah, that's just a fancy word for a sick fuck. This game isn't good for us... not at all.

Calvin strolled over to a metal filing cabinet that sat in the corner of the room. The latch clicked, and he quickly pulled a drawer open. I watched as his blood-stained gloves thumbed through the files, leaving red droplets on every tan folder.

"Oh, here's a good one," Calvin said and whipped out the folder.

This can't be happening!

"She won her first blue ribbon four months ago in a local chili cook-off. She was gonna enter to be on 'Chopped Jr,' but well..." He held the folder up in his hand and let out a little sigh,

"You killed her. So let's go with an easy one. What is her name?" Calvin asked.

My eyes fell upon the monster. I was looking for some sign of fear or worry, but what I got instead was a smile. His head tilted back, and he released a dry laugh from his lips, followed by a few coughs.

"Does her death amuse you?" Calvin asked.

"Yes, but that's not what I'm laughing at," the monster said.

"Oh, no?" Calvin asked with an eyebrow raised.

"I just thought about what your face is going to look like when I force-feed you your pretty little girlfriend," the monster said.

I shook my head, "I'm not—" My words were cut off by the monster's roar.

"I don't fucking care about your labels. I'm gonna make him eat your face until he—" Then the monster got cut off or got something cut off. Blood started to spurt from the red chunk of meat where his right thumb used to be. Calvin stood there with the bloody scalpel in his hand and dark red drops of blood in his beard. The hair caused the blood to look far thicker than it normally did as it ran along the curls of his beard and dripped onto the floor between his feet. The thumb, a thick white hotdog-looking piece of meat, rolled off the table and landed in a puddle of blood that was filling up the floor. That light splash set off a flood of screams and curses from the monster's lips.

"So sorry, Mr. Connors, the answer we were looking for was Amber, Amber Stone," Calvin said, shaking his head as he started walking back to the file cabinet. "Hopefully, you'll do better with the next one."

"My fucking finger! You cut off my fucking finger!" the monster roared.

"I cut off your thumb, let's not be overdramatic now," Calvin replied.

He's going to kill us when he finds out.

No he won't, he loves us.

Get your head out of your ass. He's in too deep; there's no turning back now, and if he asks about Dallas-

"Shut up!" I screamed, and Calvin looked at me. He smiled and started thumbing through another set of folders.

"Don't be rude, Sarah, we want him to scream. Remember, it's the whole reason he's here," Calvin said.

My heart felt like a death row inmate trying to break out of the cage that was my chest. I stood there, watching him slowly moving, brushing blood along each bit of paper he passed.

"I like this one," Calvin said as he pulled out another folder, "You killed her with a tire iron. Cracked her skull and crumbled her eye socket. When all she did was offer to help you with your broken-down car." Calvin's jawline tightened as he softly said, "What she didn't know was your car was fine, and what you didn't know is, she was going to visit her... blank." This time, Calvin tossed the folder to the floor as he walked over to a silver tray that stood alone at the bottom of the operating table. Off that tray, Calvin picked up a cordless buzz saw. His finger pulled back on the trigger, and the grinding metal sound made me jump. Calvin smiled and said, "Here, you have a turn."

Just say no. Tell him this is making you sick. Y'all had sex; tell him the baby is under too much stress.

No!

You're right, he's crazy; you better just take the saw.

The saw weighed down my hands. I stared at it as I started walking toward the table. There was a black handle with a safety trigger and then the main trigger at the bottom. Both had to be pressed to make the saw spin. Calvin walked back over to the monster and leaned down, staring into his eyes.

"Who was she going to visit? Come on, this one is easy. You followed these girls for days, right?" Calvin asked softly.

The monster's eyes were so still and cold as they stared into Calvin's hazel eyes. I got closer with the saw, debating what I wanted to do with it. I could just kill him and put an end to it all. I could cut him so deeply he would fade away before we got to Dallas' file, but then again, Calvin could patch him up to keep the game going.

There is another option.

Is there?

Oh, yes.

Oh! No, no, no. We can't do that.

They're both crazy, far more unfit to live than we are.

I don't think Calvin is crazy he's just-

"Caroline, Caroline Parker." The monster's voice froze my blood. I watched as Calvin stood up, still glaring at the monster as he continued, "She was blonde, maybe seventeen or sixteen. She also talked way too much, but then again, that could have been because of the fear. They all seem to talk a lot when they're scared. Begging, pleading, just yapping like little puppies," the monster said.

"Who was she going to see?" Calvin asked.

"Her grandmother," the monster said.

I turned on the saw, and Calvin shook his head, putting up his hand.

"His right," Calvin said, and the metal buzzing of the saw stopped. This game was making me feel uneasy, not because of the sound of the saw, but because it had to stop. This was truly a game, one with actual rules. Calvin was doing some kind of fair play with this monster, and that made me feel... uneasy. A fair man was a sane man, and a sane man was no help to us.

"I helped her. Just like I helped all of them," the monster said. His head rolled over to the side, and his eyes fell on me; he smiled.

We're gonna have a room right next to his.

"It's heartbreaking to watch them try and live a normal life —" The monster was cut off by Calvin's fist slamming into his mouth. I watched as the blood started to pour from his lip, then darker blood started to push from his mouth as he started coughing. The monster's head turned to the side, and he let out a loud, blood-filled cough. The splatter stained my white apron, and a small object slapped into my stomach. I leaned down to pick it up; it was covered in blood and very jagged, but I knew for sure what it was.

It's his tooth.

"You only speak when spoken to!" Calvin shouted.

Who's more of a threat? Who's more of a risk to our lives?

What do you mean?

The monster can kill us, or maybe not, but Calvin can lock us away forever. There's no doubt about that. We will never see the light of day.

Calvin turned toward the cabinet once again. This was becoming a pattern. His gaze would fall upon the cabinet, and my heart would start seizing up. He would describe a bloody encounter with the monster, and I would pray it wasn't Dallas. The monster got used to the game as well. He started spitting out correct answers, never lying or dancing around the question. He was a perfect little saint. I kept my eyes on Calvin as he thumbed through the folders that held all this power and knowledge. Little bits of paper that seemed to hold the whole lives of the monster's victims.

Shit.

What?

This game. It only works because the doctor has the answers in those folders.

And?

And! If the answers are sweet little nuggets of knowledge about those dead girls then-

Then he knows!

He knows you're lying about Dallas.

No he couldn't know. I mean, why do this if he knows?

Why do this at all? Because he's crazy!

I listened for Calvin's blood-covered gloves to start pushing the folders along their track, and when that sound came, I took my first steps toward the monster. He was a beast that stole my sweet Dallas away from me. A beast that had stolen other sweet girls from the world. And even in this broken state, he still had the power to steal something else from me. The beautiful world I had created with Dallas. He could twist my hours of watching her into something dark and depraved. This monster could open his lips and cast me as an insane woman who created a fairytale life with some random girl. Even strapped to a table, the monster had far too much power, and he knew it.

Kill him!

The chilling buzz started again as I moved toward the monster. I could see Calvin's head turn. He was screaming something, but the buzzing filled my head. The buzzing was all I could hear. The blade crept closer to the monster, and I could see him frantically tugging and pulling at his straps. The fear that I had been waiting for was finally here. I imagined this was the look that my poor Dallas had on her face. I couldn't see her eyes, but I pictured this was what she looked like when that rope went around her neck. She was scared. No, she was terrified of that monster.

But now he's terrified… of us!

Yes!

Kill him!

As the saw started to get closer, I could feel Calvin racing toward me. He wanted some form of justice, or maybe he just wanted to see me suffer as he prolonged my fear of hearing Dallas' name. I wasn't sure what was running through Calvin's mind, but I knew what was racing through my own. I wanted this to end. I wanted to walk away from this clean and without worries, like Calvin promised. I felt the bloody hands tightly grab me from behind. It wasn't the sweet touch around my waist that he placed upon me earlier; no, this was not the embrace of a lover. As my body twisted and started to fall, I could see the look in Calvin's eyes was that of a mad man. The saw fell forward, and with its final rotation, it sliced through the monster's wristbands and shattered, sending a large black shard into the middle of the monster's hand.

"What the hell do you think you're doing!" Calvin roared.

I was not using him. This was not my master plan of unleashing revenge for a murdered obsession. No, that might have been the carrot that he dangled in my face, but it was Calvin who was pulling all the strings. He used us to play out his sick little fantasies on a soul no one will miss. I stared into his eyes, the once hazel balls of beauty and love. I stared into them, and all I could see was hate. I was so lost in my fear that I didn't see the monster free himself until he was upon Calvin, biting into his neck like a rabid dog.

Get up! Get up!

I sprung to my feet and took off running for the door. I looked back only once, to see Calvin tossing the monster down onto the floor and flipping the operating table onto him.

"Sarah!" Calvin roared.

I ran through the doorway and slammed the door. My fingers trembled and fought to find the right key.

"Sarah!" Calvin hollered.

My heart was pounding. The metal jingled as I tossed the keys along the ring.

Hurry!

Wrong one.

Hurry!

Wrong one!

Sarah!

And then, by the grace of God, the key slid in and the lock turned. I saw the door shake as something came crashing into it. I stumbled backward into the wall and slid down until I was sitting with my knees tightly pressed to my chest. There was a monster and a madman, fighting in a cage. An old cage that would only hold for so long. Soon one of them will escape, and what will that mean for me?

I don't know.

What do you mean you don't know? You said you could help!

I'm confused. Can you tell me the story again?

I've already told you it five times now!

Just one more time and this time tell it really, really slow.

Fine...

"Calm down, Sarah" Dr. Alexander's soothing voice broke through my internal turmoil. His warm, dark hand rested on my golden brown fist, and his finger gently rubbed along my skin, as if trying to extract the anger...

SHADES OF BLUE (FIRST PUBLISHED IN VOICES OF ROMANCE)

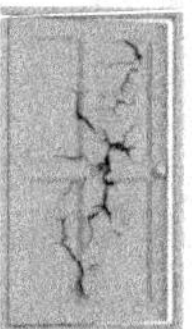

"My brand is my baby... My brand is my baby."

Do you know what a daily mantra is? They're those little sayings you repeat to yourself, and by speaking them into the universe, they're supposed to manifest into your destiny or something like that. Every morning, my sister Isabella sends me a new one. It's been two years of 3 AM 'Go get 'em, Boss Bitch' texts, and the only things I've gotten are coffee and lunch orders. I used to pick up breakfast for the office, but someone claimed they were allergic to bacon and requested I no longer do the breakfast orders.

"My brand..."

No one is allergic to bacon. Even a pig will eat a pig if you give it a chance.

"Is my baby!" I shouted.

The reason I'm here, yelling at my bathroom mirror at this ungodly hour, is because "No Bacon Becky" called out this morning and told me to cancel all her meetings. She only had one meeting on the books, and I didn't want to be rude... okay, I'm trying to steal a client and get off of coffee duty. Sue me!

The phone vibrated so fiercely in my hand that I jumped and almost dropped it.

"Get a grip, Mia," I whispered.

I combed my fingers through my hair and saw the message come to life as I got dressed for the victory that was in my near future.

LIL SIS: You got this chica! Show them you mean business, who's the client? Is it Drake? Slip him my number! No! Face-Time me!

I rolled my eyes and tried my best not to laugh, calling attention to myself as I made myself at home in Bacon Becky's office. My fingers danced along the screen:

ME: Damn! Can I reply Hoe?
    Lil Sis: My B :-)
    Me: It's not Drake, we handle movie and tv talent.
    Lil Sis: Drake did tv... duh!
    Me: ITS! NOT! DRAKE!!!!
    Lil Sis: Okay! Who is it?

"REBECCA GOLDMAN?" He asked. It was a smooth question, laced with a hint of dominance in his tone.

My head slowly came up from my lap as I awkwardly settled into Rebecca's black leather chair. All her planner said was 'Blue 11:30!!!'. I watched in awe as his hand extended towards me, his white gold Rolex peeking out, gently tucked beneath a bright white cuff of his tan, fitted suit.

"Vincent... Vincent Grant. I'm sorry, I'm late," he said.

I looked back down at my phone and then tossed it into the open desk drawer before standing up, perhaps a bit too eagerly, to shake his hand. He had a firm grip... he must work out.

"It's fine; I was just dealing with one of my other clients. You know how it is?" Why did I say that? What am I talking about?

Vincent politely smiled and sat down across from me. "You don't need to explain. My manager had a few fires to put out back in the day."

He had a clean haircut that made his brown hair shine under the office lights, like he was stepping out of a GQ ad. His face wasn't like those pretty boys you see trying to get into downtown clubs with their shirts unbuttoned down to their belly buttons. No, he had a rugged look, kind of like James Dean, a classic type of cute.

"I'm sure you were nothing but trouble back then," I replied.

Vincent lifted his right leg, resting his ankle on his knee. "Oh, the trouble never stopped... the manager just died."

He locked his bright blue eyes on me, but he wasn't smiling, not even a cute smirk. I had a hard time deciding if he was joking or if I should've sent out flowers.

"I'm so sorry," I mumbled.

"Don't be, it was twenty years ago. I'm sure he's come to terms with it by now," this time he laughed, and I quickly joined in. He shook his head and rested his hands on his leg, "You look nothing like I thought you would."

Was that a compliment or an insult? "And how did you think I looked?"

"Um, not that I have a problem with it or anything. My ex-wife was from Cuba. You just didn't sound Hispanic on the phone," he replied.

I raised an eyebrow at his words, and then my phone buzzed in the desk, pulling me back to what I was doing; I was building my brand, securing my destiny.

"Oh... I'm so sorry for the confusion," I laughed and wiped my sweaty palms down my pant leg.

This was the point of no return. The moment that decides whether I hear a 'Great Job, Mia! Welcome to the big leagues.' or 'You're fired! Clean out your desk and make sure you leave your business cards.' Damn, I'm going to have to take that dumb unemployment class again.

"Rebecca couldn't make it today. I'm covering her meetings, did she not tell you?" Yes! When in doubt, toss Becky under the bus and make sure she hits every wheel.

"No, no, she didn't," Vincent's demeanor changed, and I glimpsed myself filling out job applications while eating ice cream for breakfast and watching 'The Real' in my PJs. "Guess that just drives home the point I was making."

"What point was that?" I asked.

"The trouble never stops," he smiled and uncrossed his legs. I watched the tan fabric begin to unwrinkle as my dreams imploded.

"I can help you with all your needs, Mr. Grant," I couldn't let him leave. I couldn't let him walk out on me. "Just let me know what they are."

He smiled, sat down, and crossed his legs once again. And just like that, I landed my first client. I had no idea how big of a client he was. Mr. Grant... I mean Vincent, had a running joke where he asked me if I even really worked for the agency. Honestly, my level of cluelessness about his career was embarrassing. Thankfully, Netflix, Google, and Isabella exist.

LUNCH with my sister is always a treat and a chore. We've been taking care of each other ever since our mother passed away ten years ago. I'm never sure if 'passed away' is the right term, but I can't bring myself to use the other one. It makes it too real, too dark. Isabelle has no such problem; she makes it clear as day that it was a murder. She was just one of many women that went missing in the city.

The police were very hesitant to call it a serial killer, mostly for the same reasons I hate using the word murder. When you toss a label like 'serial killer' out, then it turns everything into something else. It's no longer something random. It's not something that just happens. It becomes an organized and planned deadly force of nature. One that's still out there.

We sat down on her dorm room floor with open Chinese takeout boxes and stacks of scripts sent over by agents of some big-named directors and some big-money studios. Everyone wanted Vincent for one project or another. When Hollywood found out he had returned looking for roles, it was like saying JFK came back for one more term.

"You are so damn messy; how the hell do you get any work done in here?" I asked.

Isabelle looked around at the piles of clothes and basketball gear that littered the floor before laughing.

"I work my best within the center of madness; it keeps me focused on my homework because if I'm not doing that, then I should be cleaning." She leaned back on a black bean bag and smiled as she scrolled through her phone. "And that's scarier than any mid-term."

I rolled my eyes and pulled a script off of the pile. My fingers ran over the black embroidered letters that sat on the cover page, 'Caged Bird' – a tale about a woman trapped in an abusive relationship, who finds an escape through singing in her church choir and then finds love in the arms of the choir director. I thumbed through the pages and looked up at Isabelle.

"What about 'Caged Bird'?" I asked.

"Pass," she quickly replied.

My eyebrow raised, and then I closed the script. "It's being produced by Netflix," I said.

"I know, it's a good script, but-"

"But what?" I asked.

Isabelle put down her phone and stared at me. "I don't think Vincent wants his first role in years to be the crazed, abusive husband. Not after everything that happened."

I nodded, and she returned to her phone, getting lost in the world of celebrities and basketball scores. When I finally did my homework on Vincent, like a professional should, I found out he was a big actor in the 80s and 90s. He was in a short-lived family drama. It only lasted one season, but it was enough to catapult him into teen heartthrob status. He did another show and had some supporting roles in movies. Nothing too big, Mama used to call them appetizer roles. They let the industry get a taste of you before really putting some money behind you. He got some summer blockbuster movies, one artsy picture, and then he hit the big times, the lead role in a James Cameron movie. That's where he met Hollywood Starlet and future wife, Jasmine Perez. She was the lead, and life imitates Art. They became a Hollywood 'it' couple. But sadly, Hollywood romances are just prequels to a scandal.

"What did he have to say about all that?" She asked.

My skin tightened as I did my best to pretend this story of a cop and his partner who was a talking dog fascinated me.

"Hey, Puta! I know you heard me!" She shouted.

Slamming the script down on the shaggy carpet, I hissed, "I didn't ask him about it, okay?"

"No, it's not okay." She said. Isabelle pulled her long black hair back and wrapped it up into a nice little bun. Her eyes locked on me, and she grabbed my hand. "Do you want to go back to cleaning hotel rooms?"

"What? No! That was only for the summer," I said.

I hated that job, but I had nothing else. The agency told me I couldn't start until the fall; I thought it was my big break, but until then, I still had bills.

"You know, the moment his face hits a camera, people are going to ask him what happened to Jasmine." Isabelle said, and then she grabbed one script and tossed it into my lap. "He has to be ready for the tough questions or they'll eat him alive, and if he's dinner then-"

"I know, I know... I'm dessert." I stared down at the bold black letters that sat neatly on the white page. "'Hillside?'"

"Vincent plays a Doctor who helps a nurse get revenge on a serial killer," Isabelle said. I recoiled from the white page like it was a cobra getting ready to strike. I shook my head, Isabelle placed her hand on my knee and sighed. "Don't make every-thing about her, okay?" Isabelle replied.

"Okay," I hissed.

It was sound advice, but that didn't make it easy, not for me and not for Isabelle, but thankfully we had distractions. She had basketball, and I had Vincent.

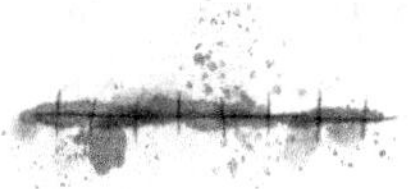

A FEW MONTHS passed after Vincent wrapped on 'Hillside'. Isabelle was right; it was an amazing role for him, and he was grateful that I brought it to his attention. So much so that he got me a new car. It was beautiful and it floored me, but it wouldn't be the last thing that Vincent gave me.

"Are you nervous?" I asked.

Vincent looked at my reflection in the mirror and smiled. "If I said I was, could we skip this and get dinner?"

I laughed and turned him around as my fingers went about their business tidying up his black tie. "No," I replied.

"No, to playing hooky or no to dinner?" He asked.

I placed my finger on my lips and leaned back, staring at him. "You should have worn the other suit. It made your eyes pop," I said.

"You're avoiding the question," Vincent replied.

"No, I'm not," I replied.

I was. As much as I tried to ignore it, there was something growing between us. I wasn't sure if it was the gratitude we felt we owed each other or that neither of us had anything that even remotely resembled a dating life.

"I like you, Vincent, but for this to work, there have to be some rules," I said.

"Rules?" He said with a playful hint of disgust.

"Yes, rules," I said and laughed.

"Like?" Vincent asked.

I wasn't expecting to be on the spot like that, but lucky for me, the show was about to start. The door opened, and a stage-hand motioned for Vincent to follow him.

"This discussion is not over," Vincent said.

When the door closed behind him, I released a trapped breath from my chest. I ran my hands over my face and did my best to pull myself back into reality. I was his agent, nothing else. Friends become lovers, and you can't do business with lovers. I saw Vincent's blue eyes and bright white smile fill up the screen, and it drew my finger to the volume button.

"So, it looks like things are looking up for you," Vincent smiled and nodded. But before he could answer and thank the fans for his comeback, the late-night host dropped a bomb on the interview. "I'm sure Jasmine would have been proud," Jimmy said.

Vincent's smile faded, and my chest tightened. It felt like I was in that chair, like it was my darkest moment being pulled up in front of the world. Vincent folded his hands together and stared at his interlocked fingers.

"I'm sure she is proud. Jasmine always wanted me to push

for more in life," Vincent's eyes came up to the camera. "This is for you, babe," he said, stealing the hearts of every woman in America.

"Yeah, that entire event was tragic... just what were you two doing that far out in the ocean?" Jimmy said.

Vincent leaned back in his seat. I got to my feet quickly and bolted through the greenroom door.

"That sneaky son of a bitch," I muttered.

This wasn't on their list of questions. It's a late-night talk show, not an Oprah interview. I pushed past the stagehands, only to make it to the set entrance. I could see Vincent lean forward and rub his hands together.

"I ask myself that every day. It was a sweet anniversary surprise. Just me and her on a boat for a weekend," Vincent said. I could see Vincent clear the tears from his eyes before he looked back at the host. "I didn't tie the boat to the dock right. It was one mistake that snowballed into another and another."

"I'm sorry, you don't have to-"

"No, I do. I want to, Jimmy," Vincent combed his fingers through his hair. "Jasmine woke up in the middle of the night and went on deck, her scream... it was like waking up to a horror movie. Sometimes I still hear it." Vincent said softly. His eyes turned toward the crowd, and a tear ran down his cheek. "I heard the scream and then slashing. I raced up to the top deck and screamed for her, but there was no answer. So I jumped in-"

"You jumped into the ocean, in the middle of the night?" Jimmy asked.

The entire set was silent. It was a story that the world had been dying to hear, and not a soul dared to interrupt it, aside from that idiotic host.

"If you lost your heart, wouldn't you do anything to get it back?" My hand instinctively went to my chest. "I was in that water until they wrestled me out of it."

The boat rental company reported the boat missing in the

morning. That's when the coast guard went looking for Vincent and Jasmine. They found Vincent out of his mind, miles away from the boat... still looking for her. Doctors say he ruptured one of his eardrums going so deep repeatedly, but he never found her. No one has.

"You killed it!" I announced, and our glasses clinked together, the bubbles tickling my nose before dancing around my tongue, igniting a celebration in my mouth that was over twenty years overdue. The champagne glass came away from Vincent's lips, and his blue eyes locked onto mine.

"We killed it, Mia. I couldn't have done any of this without you, Mia." Vincent said.

After that interview, I realized I didn't need my firm; they were thinking too small. Vincent was a supernova in a world too blind to understand his talent, but as the song goes, 'I once was blind, but now I can see.' My skin tingled, and my heart raced as Vincent's soft skin brushed the back of my hand.

"I'm not sure how I made it this long without you," he said.

I chuckled and took another sip of my drink. "You would've been just fine without me," I replied.

"No, I really wouldn't have been," he insisted.

Our interlocked fingers sent a jolt through my body, and finally, my mind intervened to halt the roller coaster ride my heart was on.

"I'm going to the bathroom," I said.

"I'll order us another bottle," he offered.

I laughed and grabbed my purse from the counter. "You do that."

As I navigated through the joyful laughter and drunken slurs that filled the bar, I couldn't help but appreciate the unique energy of Hollywood nightlife. It was like playing the lottery, hoping to get lucky and share a drink with a movie star, or maybe even take one home. Vincent's fifteen years my senior, which may seem odd anywhere else, but it's pretty common here.

Vincent was different, not like all the rest. Maybe it was because the town had turned its back on him, but there was something genuinely special about him, a sort of knight-in-shining-armor thing, rescuing an abandoned puppy before the city could put it down. Okay, that was a morbid analogy, but it wasn't too far off.

After making sure I was alone in the bathroom, I took a moment to reapply my lipstick in front of the mirror. Then, I closed my eyes, took a deep breath, and whispered to myself.

"I am a powerful, legitimate boss. And I deserve great things to happen to me."

As I inhaled deeply, a chill briefly tickled my nose, causing my skin to tighten. Suddenly, I felt like I was being watched, and an irrational fear washed over me. My worry about someone walking in during my personal pep talk seemed entirely justified in that moment.

"I'm so sorry," I stammered. The words escaped my lips before my eyes fully opened, but when they did, no word in my vocabulary could explain the feeling that overcame me. Dirty, wet hair clung to her face. Gray eyes leered at me through the mirror, their intensity like daggers. Her hands thrust toward her neck, clawing desperately at her throat. I watched, transfixed, as if I were trapped inside a sinful theater set ablaze. Her nails ripped into her skin, dragging flesh down in one rapid, horrifying motion. She screamed, and I was freed from her trance, bolting out of the restroom.

The door slammed into the wall, drawing everyone's attention, but I didn't care. I made a beeline for the exit, but suddenly, Vincent's powerful arms intercepted me.

"Mia? You okay?" he asked.

"Is everything alright?" a man inquired.

I looked up at Vincent, trembling, then pointed back at the bathroom. "There's a dead woman in there," I whispered.

Vincent's concerned look transformed into one of confusion. He exchanged glances with the man before returning his gaze to me. "Wait here," he said, then left with the man, both cautiously approaching the restroom.

I sat at the bar and turned my back to the curious onlookers. Their stares reminded me too much of those eerie white eyes in the mirror. My fingers clutched my glass, causing the liquid inside to sway back and forth, spilling over the edges and running down my fingers. I hadn't realized I was shaking or crying until that moment. I raised the glass to my lips and downed the cold, golden liquid that had been waiting for my arrival. Then, I finished Vincent's drink as well.

A hand gently rested on the middle of my back, and I jumped. Vincent came into view, his eyes flicking between the two empty glasses and me.

"Did you see her?" I asked, my voice trembling.

He looked at the empty glasses for a moment, then sighed, gazing up at me. "There was no one there," he said.

"No, no, that can't be. She was right..."

I pointed towards the restroom, but suddenly my hand felt so heavy. My entire body felt heavy. My lips moved ever so slightly, but I couldn't form a coherent sentence. I stood up, only to have the floor ripped out from under me as I collapsed. Vincent loomed over me, his words muffled, and then the man returned, assisting Vincent in helping me up. They both seemed so massive, like towering palm trees. The room grew darker, as if something were slowly blocking my vision, until all I could see were her pale eyes and all I could hear was her haunting scream.

PEOPLE ALWAYS SAY, 'I got so messed up, I don't even remember last night.' They say it as if it's something relatable, but I've never had that kind of night. I might drink until I need to take my heels off, maybe until I forget how to work the Uber app, or even enough to make me send a late-night text to an ex, but I've never reached the point where I couldn't remember what happened the night before... until now.

The room slowly came into focus, revealing a sea of soft, white nothingness. My body felt heavy, and even my eyelids required an enormous amount of effort to keep them open.

My palms pushed at the white fabric, only to feel a cool rush of air hit my skin as it slid down off of me and onto the floor in a heap. The sun was blinding, and I struggled against it, but I couldn't escape its relentless brightness. It shined down on every part of me, casting a harsh light on my shame that wished it could hide back under that sheet.

I sat up, and as my hands touched my bare skin, I realized there was no place for my shame to hide anymore. The weight of uncertainty filled me, and I couldn't remember how I ended up here.

Tears welled up in my eyes as I forced myself out of bed, wrapping that soft, white sheet around my body. I'm the older sister, from a single-parent Latin household. I won't judge anyone's life, but one-night stands weren't me.

The glass door unfrosted as I pulled it open, and I ventured down a long hallway, trying to piece together the events of the night before. We had drinks, or maybe just one drink, and then I went to the bathroom... I stopped, the memory of the bloody woman coming back in a rush. I tightened the sheet around me and closed my eyes, attempting to shake off the chill that surrounded me.

I pushed past the image of that woman and her haunting scream, only to be left with darkness, punctuated by blurred moments of confusion. Muffled words and hazy faces filled my thoughts.

I sighed and opened my eyes to catch sight of a woman in a black dress turning the corner ahead of me.

"Excuse me," I called out to her, but she didn't respond. It irritated me when people couldn't spare a moment to acknowledge another human being. It drove me crazy. My bare feet slapped along the wooden floors as I quickened my pace behind the woman.

"Excuse me!"

She stopped at the end of another hall, and I tugged at my white sheet to ease its drag on the floor.

"Thank you, where—"

Before I could finish my sentence, the woman suddenly turned right and bolted down the hallway. "What the hell!"

I balled up the remaining portion of the white sheet and chased after her, looking like a THOT Bride-to-be. on a wild adventure. But as I turned the corner, I collided with a set of muscular arms and a chest that concealed a heart I'd been yearning to know.

"You okay?" Vincent asked.

"No! No, I'm not okay!" His hands moved from my hips to my shoulders, and I quickly recoiled. All feelings of longing and puppy love fantasies vanish when you wake up naked with no memory of what went on. "What the hell happened!"

"What do you..." Vincent glanced at my makeshift toga and then raised his hands defensively. "Nothing happened. You passed out, and I brought you here to make sure you didn't die."

"That's what hospitals are for." We locked eyes for a moment, his filled with concern, mine filled with confusion and contempt.

"Listen, let's start over. I was making breakfast." Vincent said, the last part delivered with a hopeful smile, as if a meal could erase the weirdness of the situation…. But I wondered if he made pancakes.

I crossed my arms over my chest, holding the sheet tightly around me. "I can't find my clothes," I mumbled.

"They're in the wash, but there's a closet full of things you can wear until they're done," he replied.

"Why did you wash my clothes?" I questioned.

"To get rid of the evidence," he said, and a weak smile followed.

It was meant as a joke, the kind my younger self would have giggled at and brushed off, but years of loss and disappointing dates had stifled the immature laughter out of me.

Vincent smiled and rubbed the back of his neck. "If I knew this was how you acted after a night of drinks, I would have suggested sushi instead," he quipped.

I ran my fingers through my hair and sighed. "Just give me my phone so I can call an Uber," I demanded.

"You really don't remember last night, do you?" Vincent asked.

"No, I don't remember a damn thing!" I snapped.

Vincent's jaw tightened, and he pulled what looked like my phone's demonic cousin out of his pocket. I held my hand out, and the twisted metal and shattered glass phone was reluctantly surrendered to me.

"You broke it when you were running out of the bathroom," he explained.

"I did this?" I whispered, my disbelief mirrored by the phone's cracked screen.

The phone looked like a pack of wild elephants salsa danced

on it... do elephants live in packs? Stay focused! My eyes reluctantly left the phone and met Vincent's icy blue gaze.

"You want to tell me what that was all about?" he inquired.

"The only thing I want to do is go the fuck home!" I exclaimed.

I didn't care about his feelings or how adorable his eyes looked in a state of confusion. I didn't care about what he thought of me or what the hell had happened in that bar bathroom. All I cared about was getting home and leaving this bizarre night behind me. I clutched the white sheet tightly to my chest.

"I just want to go home, Vincent, please," I pleaded.

Vincent's eyebrows furrowed before he rolled his eyes and turned his back to me. I watched him walk through the living room and into an adjacent room. With my eyes closed, I ran my fingers through my hair, trying to collect my scattered thoughts.

"Shit," I muttered under my breath.

This was it. This was the end of everything. Once word got out about this meltdown, no one is gonna want to work with me, well no one worthwhile. I might get those performance artists from downtown. You know the ones that paint themselves gold and do the robot. I dropped onto the couch and let out a deep sigh, my gaze shifting to the massive TV mounted on the wall. I bet it cost as much as my rent, he's watching a tv that cost over three months of my rent.

I dropped onto the seat and let out a deep sigh, my gaze shifting to the massive TV mounted on the wall. Just before the screen came to life I saw her, the same woman in black that I chased through these halls. I could see her reflection, leaning in as if whispering something into my ear. But then the darkness on the screen vanished, replaced by the local news.

::THANK you for tuning into Wake Up Nevada, I'm John-::

. . .

My unease grew as as I searched for that woman who seemed to play hide and sneak with me, whether I wanted to be a part of her creepy game or not. I was almost ready to leap to my feet and chase her down once again, but then the words coming from the tv hit me, like a brick, smashed into my skull.

"Nevada?" I whispered.

A chill ran down my spine, and even as I tried to pull my hands away, they seemed magnetically attracted to my skin. It was as if I were too afraid to touch anything or be touched. My body moved almost involuntarily, rising from the black leather seat, and I slowly made my way in the direction Vincent had disappeared.

I peeked my head into the room to find him standing in a large kitchen beside a black granite island. His cell phone was resting on the granite, the only object in the room that held his attention.

"Why does that TV say we're in Nevada?" I blurted out.

Vincent didn't look over at me; instead, he swiftly grabbed his phone and shoved it into his pocket.

"Because we are in Nevada. The Black Rock Desert, to be more precise," he replied calmly.

"The desert?" I muttered, puzzled.

"You're not gonna scream again, are you?" Vincent asked, his tone laced with sarcasm.

Ignoring his comments, I rushed toward the nearest window, yanked the curtains open, and was greeted by the surreal sight of a beautiful white oasis, surrounded by miles and miles of dry desert dirt.

"What the fuck!" I shouted.

"Calm down, Mia." Vincent urged.

"No! You don't get to tell me to calm the fuck down! You

drove me to Nevada!" I accused him, my frustration boiling over.

Vincent looked away, his gaze fixated on the white kitchen floor. I took a step closer.

"What?" I demanded.

"Huh?" Vincent replied, feigning ignorance.

"Why are you looking like I kicked your damn puppy?" I snapped.

Vincent shrugged, then finally admitted, "We didn't drive out here."

"What do you mean, we didn't drive?" I asked, my confusion deepening.

Once again, Vincent attempted to avoid eye contact, prompting me to resort to a tactic I reserved for cheating boyfriends and racist co-workers at Holiday Parties; I slapped the shit out of him. I watched as his soft white skin transform into a bright pink, the outlines of my fingers were imprinted on his face.

"What the hell do you mean?" I demanded.

Vincent's hand rubbed his cheek before he hissed, "We flew here, in my chopper." His fingers slid onto the dark black countertops as his thumb tapped against the granite. "I usually fly out here when I don't want to be disturbed. The pilot is on call, but he won't be able to get here until noon tomorrow," he explained.

"Why?" I asked.

"Dust storm, no way in, no way out." Vincent mumbled.

I shook my head. There was no way this was happening. In just a few hours, I had gone from drinks with a crush to feeling like I was stuck in a bad lifetime movie. My bare feet cautiously led me to the glass door in the kitchen, where I could see a large white pool surrounded by artificial green grass reminiscent of mini-golf courses. Beyond that? Nothing. No buildings, houses, or roads. Just brown and red dirt, with our location marked by a solitary white spot in the vast emptiness.

"You should get dressed." Vincent suggested.

I looked over my shoulder for a moment and then back out at the pool.

I glanced over my shoulder for a moment and then back out at the pool. "I need to call my sister," I replied.

His eyes traced along my bare back, and then his hand rested on my shoulder. I quickly pulled away.

"Come on, get dressed, and you can call her from my phone," Vincent said.

I silently agreed and followed him. As I walked behind him, doubts filled my mind. Had I overreacted? Maybe he genuinely thought this was romantic or was trying to help. But as my uncertainty grew, Vincent began talking about the house.

"I had it built in the early '90s; it was going to be a surprise for Jasmine," he shared.

His fingers ran along the wood of a blue door, the only colored door in the house, hell everything else was glass. It was a stalker's wet dream.

"She always wanted us to get away, escape all the lights and just be free... but now it's just me." Vincent said. Sadness washed over the moment, so much so that I was forgetting my internal struggle of hating Vincent. Although, I quickly reminded myself it was far too early for Stockholm syndrome to set in.

"What's in there?" I asked, not because I cared, but just to break the tension of the moment.

Vincent's gaze lingered on the blue door, and he gently patted it. "It used to be a trophy room, but it's infested with black mold. I wouldn't go anywhere near it if I were you," he warned.

"You planning on fixing it?" I asked.

"No, there's death in that room; I just plan on keeping it locked away," he replied with a hint of laughter, a joke that I seemed to miss. "Just make sure you never go in it."

He was talking like I would be here longer than a day. I had no plans of exploring his moldy little trophy room. It was most likely some extravagant porn theater anyway. Following him back to a bedroom much like the one I had woken up in, except this bed was larger, and had black silk sheets My clothes were neatly folded on top of it. Vincent retrieved his phone and handed it to me.

"Thanks," I muttered.

Vincent nodded and began to make his way to the door. I turned to watch him leave, and as the door closed behind him, my fingers dialed like they were possessed. I put the phone to my ear and listened as it rang, and rang.

"Pick up the phone," I muttered impatiently until Isabelle's voice finally filled my ears.

"Hey, what's up?" she said cheerfully.

"Isabelle, I'm freaking the fuck out. Last night... something happened." I whispered urgently into the phone.

"What!" She shouted.

"I'm not sure, but I think Vincent drugged me, and I'm ninety-nine point nine percent sure I've been kidnapped," I confessed, taking a deep breath. "I need help," I added.

"Damn, that sucks. You know what else sucks? That I'm not here!" Isabelle replied, laughing. And then telling me to wait for the beep, but I didn't. I ended the call and immediately started dialing another number. My fingers smashed nine, one, one so hard that I thought I might break the phone's screen. I held it to my ear and glanced up, and there she was—the blood-stained woman from the bar, staring at me through the window. Her eyes were pale and milky white, her skin gray like ash. The only color she possessed was in her jet-black hair blowing in the wind and the blood running down her neck. Her lips parted, and I braced myself for her scream.

My hands shot to my ears, and I screamed, "No, no, no!"

My body tensed, anticipating that bone-chilling cry, but what I heard was far more horrifying—the faint sound of shattering glass as the phone plummeted to the wooden floor. My eyes widened, and I rushed to pick it up. When I looked back at the window, nothing was there except the scorching desert landscape. I gazed down at the shattered black mirror and tapped the screen, hoping to bring it back to life, but I got nothing. The door opened and Vincent's voice surrounded me.

"Are you alright?" He asked.

No, I wasn't alright! I was far from it. Vince kidnapped me. I was clearly suffering some mental breakdown due to whatever drug he slipped into my drink. I was either hallucinating or being haunted. Regardless, I was far from alright. My finger traced the broken black screen as I finally mustered the courage to ask a question that had been plaguing me since I had woken up here.

"Vincent, who else is here?" I asked.

I knew the answer before it left his lips, but tears still ran when I heard his answer.

"Nobody, why?" He said.

HOURS PASSED, and I found myself back in the room with the white sheets, unable to tear my gaze away from my feet, too afraid to look anywhere else. Vincent made us something to eat. I was apprehensive about being drugged or poisoned, but I figured if he wanted me dead, I would be by now. So, I ate. He spoke about our time together, about our future, using words that sounded like we were a married couple on a weekend getaway. I let his words wash over me, my focus fixed on the belief that, despite what Vincent had told me earlier, we were not alone.

As we sat at the dinner table, in chairs that should have been empty, sat women. They were all different, each one unique in her own way. Some had jet-black hair, while others were blonde. One appeared to be my mother's age, or the age she would have been now, and another looked like she wasn't even old enough to take the SATs. The only common thread among them was that they were women, they were dead, and they fixed their pale, haunting eyes on me. Throughout the entire meal, they stared at me in eerie silence, with no words, just haunting glares, while Vincent continued his declarations of love.

"Are you listening?" he asked.

The women all slowly nodded, prompting me to do the same. The night continued with a tour of the house, which was far from the open layout people seemed to prefer nowadays. Most areas were locked behind closed doors, with only the living room and kitchen open to us.

Vincent proudly showed me each room, speaking of the hours he had spent here, shaping the place to his liking. We moved from one room to another, but when he opened the doors, I didn't see the renovations or his hard work. Instead, I saw nightmarish scenes in every room. Each room held a different woman, showcasing her last moments like some morbid art gallery. Belts, fishnet stockings, purple bruises from fingers around their throats—they all bore signs of unimaginable violence. These women were dead and locked away from the world behind these doors. Vincent didn't seem to see them, not in their state of death, and I doubted he ever truly saw them when they were alive. He overlooked them. Their fear and screams didn't matter, just as I didn't matter.

As I stared down at my feet, I remembered the one room that didn't house a ghost from Vincent's past, or maybe it did, but he didn't give me the chance to peek behind it. It was the room with the blue door, the one Vincent told me to never go into. He gave it a mask of deadly black mold. That would steal my life away, but I knew that was a lie. My eyes met the gaze of the pale-eyed woman in the room, her fingernails broken from her desperate attempts to escape. I had waited for hours, and now, in the dead of night, I stood up, looking at her.

"Now?" I asked.

She nodded slowly. I exited my room and walked down the hall. In front of each door stood a dead woman, each whispering the lies they had been told:

"I can make you famous."

"I'll show your work to my agent."

"It won't hurt."

"I can make it worth your while."

"I need you."

"I want you."

"I love you."

Then I reached the blue door, the one that lacked a ghostly occupant. The one I believed to be my room in this house of horrors. I grasped the handle and twisted, but it didn't move. It was locked, concealing its secrets from the world. I turned back to see the women all pointing down the hall toward the kitchen. Leaving them behind for a moment, I returned with a large chef's knife. I stared at the brass doorknob, feeling it sinfully whispering to me.

The victims of Vincent's past surrounded me, but their presence didn't make me feel as crazy as the haunting whisper from behind the blue door did. It wanted me to enter, to see beyond its outer shell and discover the darkness within. I rammed the knife between the door and the frame, hearing the alarming crack of splintering wood. Part of me worried that the noise would wake the monster, but I had come too far to turn back now.

With a flick of my wrist, I heard the satisfying click as the lock released. Slowly, I pushed open the blue door. My heart pounded, something about this room was pulling at my soul, despite the feeling that entering it would mean never leaving again.

As I entered, ghostly hands of a dozen women rested on my shoulder, urging me forward into the dimly lit room. This room was unlike the others; it had gray cement-blocked walls, blood-stained checkered tiles, and drains along the floor. Mounted on the walls were the wide-eyed faces of women who had walked these halls before me. I forced myself to look into their eyes, each one begging to be seen. When I reached one face, it was all too familiar—she used to stare at me from magazine covers and billboards. Her hair was jet black, and marks marred the base of her neck, unlike the others. Her stare held panic and sadness. She was the woman from the bathroom, from my bedroom, and from one of Hollywood's biggest mysteries.

"Jasmin?" I whispered softly, careful not to wake the dead, though it seemed they never slept in this blue hell, that doubled as the devil's workshop.

The ghostly hands continued to push me along the tiled floors, past swings, straps and other objects some people used to spice up their relationships, but I knew they weren't for love, not in the hands of this monster. The weight of the ghostly women rose off of me. Their need for me to see now gone. My eyes fell upon a table covered by a sheet, a lumpy shape concealed beneath it. My trembling fingers reached out, grab-bing the sheet and tossing it aside. And there she was—Isabelle, strapped to the table, stripped down to her underwear. Tears welled up in my eyes, my hands cupping her cheeks.

"Isabelle!" I cried, shaking her gently. "Isabelle!"

I worked frantically to undo the straps, then lifted her into a seated position. I pressed my ear against her chest and heard her heart beating faintly against her ribcage.

"Come on," I urged, hooking her arm around my neck and dragging her along the bloodstained floor. When I reached the blue door, I could see it—a red dot hovering just above the door, shifting from side to side like the devil's eye, keeping a vigilant watch over his trophy room.

"Come on!" I shouted, desperately trying to rouse my sister back to the land of the living. But she remained limp, a dead weight in my arms as I fought to carry her through the gates of hell. I rushed us through the blue doorframe, and when I turned, I saw Vincent staring down at a blue screen.

His icy blue eyes rose from the screen and locked onto Isabelle and me. He tapped the screen, extinguishing the light and disappearing back into the darkness of the hall.

"I gave you one rule, Mia. One." He said.

I turned and rushed down the hall toward the white room.

"One simple rule, and you broke it, just like all the others," I could hear his footsteps calmly approaching from behind. "But I'm not all that surprised. Women come from a long line of sinners, from Delilah's costly deception to Eve's questionable appetite," he said.

Finally, I reached the white room, pushing the door open and slamming it shut behind us. Frost crept across the clear glass, and I twisted the lock.

"Disobedience is in your DNA, Mia. I shouldn't have thought you were any different from the others," Vincent said.

I did my best to block out his psychotic monologue and focused on pushing a dresser in front of the door. With the knife clenched in my hand, I shoved the dresser across the floor and wedged it against the door. Suddenly, I heard him knocking lightly, calmly.

"What the hell is this, Vincent! What the hell did you do to my sister?" I demanded.

The knocking paused for a moment. I stood still, staring at the frosted glass, and then it shook under the thunderous force of a madman.

"Let me in, Mia. We can talk about it," he said.

"Stop!" I screamed.

"Let me in!" he hollered.

I held up the knife, pointing it at the door.

"Just leave us alone!" I shouted.

The tip of the knife shook frantically before me, my hands unable to stay still as the pounding on the glass continued. Each thump sent my heart leaping out of my chest.

"Let me in, you stupid cow!" Vincent screamed.

The glass exploded onto the wood of the dresser and there he stood, staring through the shattered remains of my sanctuary. His foot landed on the broken glass as he pulled himself up by grabbing onto the remaining shards of the door's frame. He didn't flinch as the glass sliced into his skin, his eyes never wavering from me, filled with the cold intensity of the ocean.

"What are you going to do with that?" he asked, dismissing me entirely. It wouldn't have mattered if I held a gun or dynamite; he wouldn't have feared me more than a child with a water gun. In his eyes, I wasn't a person or an opponent—I was merely the next head to adorn the wall of his trophy room.

"Just let us go, Vincent. I won't tell anyone, I swear. You can let us go and we'll never see each other again." I begged.

"But I enjoy seeing you," Vincent said, a sinister smile spreading across his face. Bloody footprints marked his path along the floor.

I raised my knife higher, pointing the trembling blade at his face.

"Why are you doing this?" I asked.

"Why? Why?" he mocked.

Vincent glanced to the side, his eyes falling on my sister's bare back.

"Don't you fucking touch her!" I shouted, rushing toward him with the blade.

My battle cry did little except let him know I was coming. He seized my wrist and shook it fiercely until the knife fell, scattering across the floor.

"I'll tell you why!" he roared, spinning me around and wrapping his arms tightly around me, holding me close to his chest. "I do this for the hearts that you've broken and the ones you will break. With your lies and your games." He inhaled deeply, his nose brushing my hair. "But mostly and most importantly, I do this..." His hands gripped my shoulders, and then he violently threw me to the floor.

My face bashed into the tile, blood mingling with my black hair. He tore open the back of my dress, then spun me around. His hand reached for his belt while the other gripped my bloodied face.

"Because I can," he hissed.

The belt came off, and the black leather quickly coiled around my neck, like a snake would its prey, before squeezing the life out of it. My hands shot up, and I rammed by nails into his neck, tearing at his skin. The belt tightened. My shouts became whispers. That's when the air felt like sandpaper in my chest.

The devil sought a new victim a few months ago, and unknowingly, I offered up my sister and myself to him. Through fading vision, I could see Vincent's wicked smile. He smeared my blood across his lips, forming a sinister grin.

"I love you!" he shouted as the belt tightened. "I love you!"

My hands slapped at his wrist.

"I love-"

The leather noose loosened around my neck, and I gasped for air, greedily inhaling as much as I could. Blurriness faded from my sight, revealing Vincent's wide eyes and blood-smeared lips.

His hands reached for the black handle of the large knife buried deep deep into the spot where his neck and shoulder meet. His fingertips brushed against the handle, but another set of hands forced the blade in deeper.

Isabelle loomed behind Vincent, and behind her stood a

dozen of his victims. Their hands rested on Isabelle's as she yanked the blade forward, ripping it from his neck. Blood rained down on me, and Vincent stumbled to the side, releasing me from his grip.

His hand clutched his neck, crimson slicked fingers attempting to force the blood back where it belonged, but I didn't care about that. What mattered was the look of pure terror in his wide eyes, and I knew that those Vincent had overlooked and discarded had finally gotten what they longed for.

"Do you see us now?" I whispered.

They hovered over him as Isabelle helped me to my feet. The dresser slowly eased away from the door.

"What the hell?" Isabelle said.

I smiled and embraced her tightly. "Movie magic, just movie magic.

Vincent's screams continued to echo through the house for the rest of the night, and they echo through my dreams till this day. But, you know what? That scream is the most empowering sound anyone will ever hear.

QUICK BITE: CAMP LANIER (FLASH FICTION INSPIRED BY GEORGIA'S LAKE LANIER)

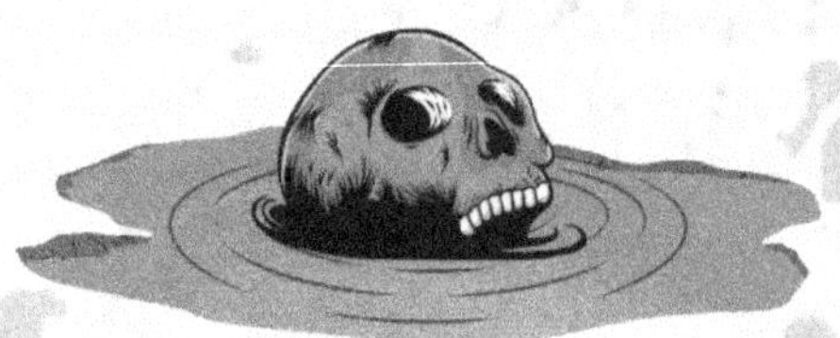

This summer, I got a chance to go to Camp Lanier, a summer camp focused on reconnecting kids with nature. To tell you the truth, I hate nature. I would have been happier spending my summer in a video game and sugar induced coma. But my mom, a single parent in need of a babysitter, had other plans for me. So, off to camp I went, armed with bug spray and lined up on a dock, awaiting my swimming lessons.

"This is a satanic sacrifice, they're tossing us into the abyss," someone whispered in my ear. The sheer terror in his voice told me it was Maxwell, who spent all of lunch informing us of the moral and legal injustices of making someone learn to swim against their will.

"You'll be fine, Max," I assured him.

Maxwell crossed his arms, his face tattooed with anxiety. "Fine? People die like this all the time. Who lines people up and makes them jump into dangerous waters? Pirates, that's who!" he hissed.

"So, you think a camp of pirates is plotting to teach kids how to swim?" I asked, trying not to laugh.

"When you say it like that, it sounds crazy," Maxwell mumbled.

"It sounds crazy no matter how I say it," I replied. We shuffled along with the other kids, the sounds of splashing and giggles up ahead serving as our backdrop to this summer time madness.

"He's not wrong," a soft voice came from the girls' line next to us. I glanced over to see a pair of hazel eyes and a dark, puffy Afro.

"You think this is a Pirate camp too?" I asked.

"No... but that would be cool. He's right about the lake, though. It is dangerous," she replied, her words capturing the attention of the other kids as we moved along the wet wooden dock. "Before there was a camp, there was a lake, and before that... there was a town. My grandpa told me that this whole lake was once a thriving Black town. People called it Little Atlanta."

"So, this used to be a town?" Maxwell asked.

"Yeah, the KKK didn't like a town of black citizens thriving, so one night they came in and murdered everyone. Grandpa said blood stained the streets when it was all said and done." The girl grabbed her big puffy Afro and held it tightly as she removed the green band from her wrist and wrapped it around her hair making a tight smaller puff on her head. "They tried to burn the town after. They lined the bodies up in the church and set them ablaze, but only the bodies burned."

"What do you mean?" I asked. I wasn't buying it. Things like this didn't happen.

"They tried setting the church on fire but it wouldn't burn, the flames would just crawl along the wood like little glowing worms and then die out. Same with all the other buildings.

Nothing would burn that night or any other time they returned with or without their hoods." She replied.

"Creepy," Maxwell said, clearly unsettled.

"What's creepy is what the state did after," she continued.

"What did they do?" I asked.

"I don't wanna go in there!" A boy suddenly screamed, grabbing our attention. His eyes were locked onto mine. Sweat poured down his face, and his heart pounded just as fast as mine.

"Kid, get in the water," our counselor, Adam, ordered.

"We shouldn't, you know that!" the boy cried, still staring at me. "They know that!" he screamed.

"Okay, enough!" Adam shouted, pushing the boy into the dark waters of the lake. The boy's screams filled my ears until... silence. "Next!" Adam called out.

"Next? He needs help, he's drowning!" I shouted.

"Everyone is," Maxwell whispered.

And as if nothing happened, the girl continued her story. "They wanted to demolish the town and hide what they did. They brought in bulldozers and dynamite, but it all failed." The girl looked over at me, "So, they drowned it. The state turned Little Atlanta into a nice sweet lake... except nothing's sweet about this place." We looked forward and the line that once felt miles long, was now at its end. We were next, "There's blood all over that town. In the soil, in the walls and in the water."

"Next!" Adam shouted.

"There's blood in the water," she whispered.

Adam's voice snapped me back to reality. "I said you're next, boy!"

turned toward him, but his eyes were now a sinister blood red. I frantically backed up bumping into the ice cold skin of the girl.

"If you know all this, why would you come here?" I asked.

"I wouldn't," she replied. But when I turned around,

everyone had vanished—Maxwell, Adam, the girl, even the sun. I was left alone in the cool darkness of the night, with the sound of water smacking against the dock.

I took a deep breath and noticed the cabin lights in the distance. I could hear faint laughter. My sweaty hands ran over my face, and I sighed deeply. I turned towards the water, cautiously inching closer to the dock's edge. I felt like I was on fire, my sweat pouring freely. I got on my knees and muttered, "I hate camp."

As I dipped my hand below the water's surface and splashed my face, a set of blood-red eyes suddenly appeared in my rippled reflection. Gray hands shot up and grabbed my arm, and a deep, demonic southern accent emanated from my haunted reflection.

"Didn't they tell you… there's blood in the water, boy!" he screamed before pulling me into the chilling depths below, where more grey hands and blood-red eyes awaited.

ABOUT THE AUTHOR

Hey Survivor!

My name is Sylvester Barzey and I am a best selling horror and fantasy author. I grew up in Bronx, NY, lived in the smallest state in the country for a while and then transplanted to Lawrence, GA.

I'm a military veteran with an addiction to all things horror. My overall goal is to shine a spotlight on BIPOC characters within the horror/fantasy genre. From a young age I was obsessed with horror movies, mostly slashers. The mythos of the "Final Girl" trope was always something that appealed to me. The act of taking someone and watching them overcome the greatest odds to be the ultimate survivor has been a strong attraction to the horror for me.

But, what I didn't realize growing up was all these survivors were White. Seeing only one type of person rise, builds blocks within people's minds, it causes them to think that surviving is a trait only in one race, which is far from the truth. The Black community (Black Women for sure) have survival built into their DNA. History has shown us that overcoming great odds is something Black people have always done.

Being that I couldn't find the final girls I was looking for (There are some don't get me wrong and they are amazing), I set out to create them. I want to produce Black heroes who overcome world shattering events and rise above them. My goal is for people to say Catherine Briggs' name in the same breath as they say Sidney Prescott and Laurie Strode. It's my mission to change horror so that my children can look at it and see themselves as survivors.

Random Facts:

I love The Golden Girls

I wonder what people taste like

I hate the snow

My Top Five Movies Are:

Scream, Candyman, Day of The Dead, Train To Busan & Mulan

Reach out to me by Author@sylvesterbarzey.com or visit his www.sylvesterbarzey.com

facebook.com/authorsylvesterbarzey

twitter.com/sylvesterbarzey

instagram.com/sylvesterbarzey

goodreads.com/sbgoodreads

bookbub.com/authors/sbarzeybookbub

amazon.com/author/sylvesterbarzey

www.ingramcontent.com/pod-product-compliance
Lightning Source LLC
Chambersburg PA
CBHW070523160726
48003CB00004B/1679